The Empties

The Glitches Series

Book Two

By Ramona Finn

Blurb

Is survival worth any price?

Cast out of the Norm, Lib must fight for every second of life among the Rogues in the desert wasteland that is now her home, scavenging in abandoned cities known as the Empties. With the help of fellow Glitch Skye she hopes to hack the AI that will allow them to return to the city and save her family. There's just one problem: Lib's memories are missing.

Lib isn't like other Glitches. Her ability to merge with technology is causing a rift in her newfound family, and putting them in danger. Soon she'll have to choose whether to return to the Norm or stay with the people she's come to rely on in the Outside. When her desire to know the truth about herself forces her to return to the Norm, handsome Rogue leader Wolf Tracker insists on accompanying her to the lion's den.

There, she meets an old friend—but Lib is no longer sure they can be trusted. When she learns a horrifying truth about the AI and her mother's part in it, Lib is shaken to the core. Now, she'll have to decide if humanity's survival

is worth a bloody cost.

Sign up to Ramona Finn's mailing list to be notified of new releases and get exclusive excerpts!

Sign up at https://forms.aweber.com/form/81/231664481.htm

You can also find me on Facebook at

www.facebook.com/ramonafinnbooks/

Table of Contents

Chapter One

The hot air hits me in quick blasts that pick up my short hair, slapping it against my forehead and the edges of my face. I keep running. The breeze is almost enough to cool the sweat that's collected at the base of my neck and where the biogear connects to me through my skin. The tiny screen above my left eye flashes a warning. Drones fly close behind me—right where I want them. I push myself to run faster, legs pounding, breaths short and fast. The biogear makes it possible. Still, my body burns with the effort.

I don't bother to glance behind and confirm what the biogear is telling me. The drones, sent out by the AI…by Conie…hum with a soft whine. I feel no fear as I might have once when facing the machines the AI uses to try and spy on us. I am no longer scared. This is a war. One I'm determined we will win. The AI intends to leave our world —and leave nothing behind. We fight now for survival— but we need to know more about the AI. Just as she tries to know about how we intend to stop her.

And we will stop her. We must.

I can't help the surge of adrenaline that pushes me to run even faster, despite the ache starting in my left calf.

I can do this.

This is the first real trial of the biogear—gear we take from drones both old and new, ones we take down with rocks and whatever else will pull them from the sky. We take the gear and adapt it to work with our bodies. The AI once wiped my memories—but not all of them. And I know more about gear than any other Glitch ever has. Just as I know the black drones have no intelligence—the AI does not share her power. But they have gear—and we can use that to make us faster, able to see more and fight them.

I spare a glance around me—a fast scan. The canyon narrows ahead of me. Relief swells within me. I'm close. All I have to do is push a little harder and get the drones into the trap.

Studying the biogear screen, I pick out the drone that is closest. It's black, the body dusty and has not extended any arms. It is ahead of three others.

Perfect.

The biogear wraps around my back, arms extend down from it to my legs, helping me move more fluidly, letting me do more with less effort. I change direction. Instead of going into the narrowing mouth of the canyon, I head straight for one of the towering rock walls.

Behind me, the whine of the drone grows louder.

With a jump and a spin, I slam my boots into the rock wall. Small shards tumble out from beneath my feet. I push off of the wall and into the air, tucking so my feet spin over my head and I fly over the drone.

The drone is too slow to correct. It starts a turn but smashes into the rock with an explosion of black from its shell. It gives a louder whine and falls to the dust. Now we have more parts to build more biogear.

I twirl and hit the ground, landing with a jarring thud and in a low crouch that lets me face the remaining three drones. They seem almost like black shadows against the hard blue of the sky—like birds without wings, or clouds that have no softness.

Turning, I start a sprint down the narrow canyon.

The biogear lets me run longer and harder, but my side aches now. Each breath seems harder. My throat is dry. But I have to do this.

We need to know more about what the AI plans—we need the drones to connect to the AI mainframe.

And this may be the only way I ever find out what happened to Raj.

A twinge of guild catches me, wraps around my chest, but I have no time to think about Raj just now. The trap is all that matters.

Glancing up to the top of the rock walls where a few straggling bushes try to grow in the Outside, I hope that Wolf and the others are in place. But they will be. We are part of the Tracker Clan now—no longer separated as Glitches like I once was, something seemingly discarded by the AI, and Rogues, those who never were under the AI's control in the Norm. No…we are clan.

Dirt spurts out from under my heels.

An instant later, the world shifts and changes.

Suddenly I'm running on a smooth floor that is flat gray. The canyon of Outside becomes a long corridor. This is the Norm—I know it well. The AI—Conie—once sent me from it to find the other Glitches so she could destroy them. But she failed. But why am I seeing this now?

Closing my eyes, I squeeze them tight, but the image is in my mind—a corridor in the Norm. I stumble and have to open my eyes again. If I fall, I'm dead.

Now the world seems to be both the dry, brown dust of Outside and the cool, hard edges of the Norm. I see both—one with my eyes and one with my mind. Gritting my teeth, I know it's the biogear—I am seeing something from the drone's memory banks.

Panic flips my heart into an even more rapid speed. It slides into my stomach and knots it. Rocks change into doors then shift back into rocks. I am losing control of the biogear and I have no time to stop and shed it—not with drones whining close behind me and the trap looming ahead.

My boots hit a rock—not smooth, metal flooring—and I tumble, manage to tuck and roll. Dust cakes my face and mouth, but I stagger back to my feet.

My senses are in overload. I seem to be in two spaces at once—both in the Outside and also inside the Norm. Something pokes at me—something from the three drones bearing down. It is a tingle in my mind—a flutter like when I connect with the AI's systems to steal water.

It is the AI—Conie.

She is trying something new with these drones—she is coming after me.

I should have expected this.

Conie sent me to find the Glitches. I did. But I did not help her destroy them. And now the Rogues and Glitches have joined to destroy Conie.

With a low growl, I start to run again. The two images blur around me, so I use what I can hear. I hear the whirring sound of the drones, slicing through the air as they come after me. Ahead I hear a rattle of rocks sliding down.

That's it…that's the trap. Wolf and the others wait there.

I run and round the bend in the canyon—it is so narrow here my shoulders brush each rock wall. Something slams into my back, throwing me onto my face. My biogear flashes and goes quiet. It falls off me. Crawling out from under the black gear with its wires sticking out and parts added in, I see it smoking. The drones used one of their beams to try and kill me. They failed.

Wolf gives a cry—one of his long howls. Even though I know it is his voice echoing against the rocks, my skin prickles.

The Tracker Clan waits here—Rogues and Glitches. They stand and roll huge boulders down into the canyon.

Two of the boulders hit. One drone wavers, spits out blue sparks and falls to the ground. The insides of the drone are partly organic and goo spills out, reddish and shimmering. Another drone spins and heads for the top of the canyon walls and the clan. Light splashes from the black drone—a line of it as if the light from the sun was turned into a spear.

I hear a cry from one of the clan—I know that voice. Bird Sees Far has been hit by the drone's beam.

Looking up, I see Bird drop back, but Wolf stands.

I curse—a habit I'm picking up from Wolf—and push myself up to my feet. Picking up a rock, I aim for the drone and hit it—not hard enough to dent its black shell, but hard enough that it turns and starts after me again.

A rock slams down onto the drone, sending it spiraling into the canyon wall.

The third drone hesitates, then reverses itself and speeds away.

Grabbing another rock, I hit it, but it still runs—back to the AI.

It is taking the information about us back to Conie— back to the AI. Now she will know what we did here. Now she will know we are using parts of drones to make us stronger. I kick my biogear, now dead and smoldering in the sand, leaking out some of the green goo that makes it functional.

Rocks tumble down, and I look up to see Wolf heading down the canyon, following a very narrow path. He moves more like one of the big cats that hunt us and everything else in the Outside. I nod to him. Wolf glances at the biogear and then at me. His mouth is pulled down, but he stands close to me. His eyes are so very dark—and he is so much taller and stronger than me. But he makes me feel safe.

He, too, kicks my biogear and then glances at the three drones we took down—or at the two, broken black shells and the one still sparking. He looks back at me again. "Still think this gear stuff is a good idea? I don't like it."

I let out a breath and rub my neck. The biogear's disconnect stung and only I am feeling it now. "The plan worked. We got gear we need. We can make more biogear—better ones."

Wolf's mouth twists down even more. "Too many injured. Lizard fell, hurt herself. Her gear failed, too."

"Maybe it wasn't the biogear that failed. Maybe the drones had a shutdown command to test on us?"

He shakes his head. "Bird and Sorrel got hit. They were hunting us."

A cold weight settles in my chest. "And if the AI goes through with her plan to leave—to take the Norm and blast it out of the ground and go into space, how many will be dead then?"

He doesn't answer, but he knows. We'll all be dead. Taking the Norm—turning it into something that can travel into space—will strip away the air we breathe. It will shatter the ground under our feet. It will leave us without water. The losses are small today compared with what we face.

Wolf glances up at the sky. "One got away."

I nod. One drone escaped. I think back to how I could suddenly see inside the Norm as well as see the Outside for a short time.

These drones are different. I connected to them in a way that let me look into the AI's Norm, the enclosed dome where the AI keeps those humans she uses to maintain her. Where she keeps Raj—or where I hope she keeps Raj.

The AI spies on us with drones—but maybe we can spy on her now, too.

Chapter Two

It takes longer than it should to salvage parts from the drones. Wolf wants to move fast—Bird, Lizard and Sorrel need care. I won't leave without gear stripped out of the black shells. My hands are sticky now with pulling apart the drones. Two of the younger ones—Alis and Mouse—help me with the gear. Lizard wants to help, too, but Wolf sends her back on an AT, one of the wheeled vehicles we have. The ATs run on solar, but we are always short on power-storage boxes. Sometimes I find a few in the Empties, those twisted empty buildings where people once lived. But the Rogue clans have scavenged the Empties for a very long time—there's not much left.

The drones give us better gear, and power-storage boxes—I find two compact blocks that we can use. It takes time to gut the drones we took down and it's messy, worse than gutting an animal for food. But I'm satisfied we got good gear from them. We get back to the clan before dark, but Wolf nods to me and I know what he is thinking—we have to move the clan.

We have no way of knowing how much information the AI will pull from the drone that got away.

The clan lives underground—it is the only way to survive the Outside. The Norm is protected by a dome—huge and slick and metal. The Outside is wild animals and dust storms and the Empties. Moving takes even more time, but Wolf won't wait. We eat, drink a little water and pack.

Wolf's smart enough to have new tunnels already built. They're closer to the Norm, but not so close that the drones will easily find us. The clan moves at first light, taking only what each person can carry. Wolf hides the ATs at another location—no use putting all our eggs in one basket, he says, but I don't know what an egg is.

It takes most of the morning to get settled. These tunnels are like the others—narrow paths dug into the rock and widened from natural caves. One main room is for meals, two large ones for sleeping, with one for males and one for females, a storage dug out for water and food, and another one for gear—the Gear Room. I insist we keep that in place. But some of the clan looks sideways at the gear I bring back with us—they don't trust anything to do with the AI. I don't like it, either, but I see no choice. We have to have gear to fight the AI. Rocks and spears won't cut it.

And survival is everything.

After the gear is stored—my biogear along with the new parts—I head to see Croc, the clan's healer. Croc has no time to tell me much.

Croc is older than anyone else in the clan. He is not as tall as Wolf, and each season seems to put more lines on his face. His dark hair is only a fringe now around a shiny, bald head. He waves me away, but I know by how he is taking his time with herbs and creams that the wounds are not bad.

"Stay off that leg, Liz, until the full moon at the least." He waves for Lizard to leave, she limps out, but shoots me a grin as she passes me. Sorrel lies on some skins on the floor, holding a cloth to her head.

I start to turn away, but Bird's now familiar voice stops me. "The gear's getting us into trouble."

Turning to look at her, I study her. Her face is twisted in anger. She cradles one arm against her chest. The sleeve of her skin tunic shows a black hole burned through it, and below that is red, raw skin.

Croc swipes salve onto the burn, and Bird hisses and then lets out a breath. Croc knows what plants can be used to take away pain. I almost want some of that salve for my back.

Glancing at me, Bird's mouth pulls down. She tips her head to one side and the ribbons in her hair flutter. She still has a round face—a young face. Her nose is wide and flat and her thick, black eyebrows flatten right now. She gestures with an elbow, since her good hand is holding onto her injured arm. "The gear's making you reckless. You're making others that way, too, now."

I lean a shoulder against the cold rock of Croc's room. He is the only one who gets his own room, but this one really looks more like a wide tunnel with skins over each way in and out. "You know this is about survival."

"Is it? Or is it you looking for a way back into the Norm, Lib?"

Cold sweeps through me. I once thought I could be friends with Bird, but she is difficult. And her visions—the things she sees—worry me.

Her visions aren't wrong—at least they never have been so far—but I do not like the ones that say I will betray my clan.

And I know Bird thinks I bring death.

She may be right about that.

Pushing off the wall, I try to find something to tell her —but I don't know what I can say. She dislikes the biogear, won't even try it on. She moves away from Croc and shoves past me. I turn to see where Bird's going and instead see Wolf walking down the tunnel.

Bird stops in front of Wolf, and I don't have to hear her angry, muttered words to know what she is saying. She has said this before.

She hates the biogear. It's bad. It will destroy the clan.

I wish I could agree with her and bring peace, but if it is a choice between fighting the AI or just letting Conie win and kill us all, I will chose fighting every time.

Bird sweeps out a wave with her good arm, and I know she must be telling Wolf I should not be allowed to scavenge more gear. That we should dump it in the Outside.

Turning away from her, I think about what we did accomplish. We retrieved gear from three drones, including two power-storage boxes, and I will give one of those to Wolf to use in an AT. Better gear means we can do more to fight the AI.

And I have plans for new biogear—upgrades to hack the AI and maybe even turn that biogear shutdown command, if there is one, against her. Irritation with Bird that she won't see how the biogear is helping us, I turn and head for where she is still talking to Wolf.

Wolf's dark eyes shift to me. Bird cuts off her words and turns as well. I don't look at her, I look at him. His eyes always tell me more than any of his words. He is listening to Bird, giving her a hearing—and he agrees with her. But he knows what is at risk--everything.

"We should dump that gear. It's changing the clan." Bird rubs at her injured arm.

I don't flinch at her words, but face her. "Maybe the clan should change. Maybe it has to. Maybe that's the only way to stay alive."

Glancing at Wolf, I see his gaze steady on me. A sudden, desperate need for him to understand fills me. He is clan leader—if he says the biogear must go, it must. But I will go with it. I can't give up on what may be our only chance to defeat the AI.

Wolf gives a nod and looks at Bird. "You're hurt. That's not a time to make decisions." His voice is stern but not unkind.

I let out a breath. So far, he supports what I am doing. Or maybe it is just that he has no other ideas for how to fight the AI. Before I came, the clan only had to find food and water. Now it has to do a lot more.

Bird's ribbons flutter as she shakes her head. She presses her lips tight and then mutters, "I'm hurt because her plan put us all at risk. We shouldn't be playing with things we don't understand. We depend too much on gear, maybe we become too much like the AI."

I step forward. "This is what we have to do. We have to risk more…and more…and more. There's no end to this until the AI is gone—one way or another. We just have to accept that sometimes things go wrong."

Bird's eyebrows go up and her eyes go wide. "Things go wrong? No…your biogear went wrong. There are prices too high to pay, and one of them is the loss of who we are. Another is the loss of every clan member."

Wolf slashes a hand between us. "Enough. We'll talk later in council."

Turning, Bird stares at him. Her entire body seems taut —she almost hums with a need to lash out.

In contrast, I feel light-headed and tired. This is both one of the worst days I've known and one of the best—we have new gear and I want to get to it and take it apart to see how it works. I also need to clean up—I smell like chemicals right now.

Guilt tingles over my skin. Bird is not wrong when she says I want this. I do want to get back into the Norm, but only to find Raj and to maybe stop Conie. But I can't go back without a better plan or I may end up caught like Raj was.

Looking at Wolf, I wonder how he feels about all this… about me. I find it hard to read his expressions—he always seems distant. But when I'm around him, I want him to approve of what I am doing. I want…something more.

At times, he is the most important connection I've made since waking up alone in the Outside.

Wolf puts a hand on Bird's shoulder. "Go rest."

She shakes off his hand, glances at me with cold eyes and walks away.

I let out a long breath. "I think Bird needs some time away from me."

"Bird is not wrong."

Glancing up at Wolf, I smile. "No, she's not. But she's not entirely right. We need the biogear—we have to figure out the AI's next step."

"What if that gear led the drones to us?" Wolf folds his arms across his wide chest.

Swallowing, I don't know what to say. He's looking at me with something like disappointment.

Wetting my lips, I lift a hand and let it fall again. "It is possible. But...we all know the dangers. Go out when the sun is up and deal with heat and drones. Go out at night and it's the big cats who hunt you, along with other troubles to be faced. There's no good time and we need more gear. We lose at least half of each drone when we take them out." Chewing on my lip, I wonder if I should say more about what seemed like a connect to the AI—how I was suddenly both back in the Norm with my vision as well as outside.

Wolf's mouth twitches down. "We need better plans. We're not going to be able to fight the AI at all if most of the clan is hurt or dead."

I flinch at his words. They hurt like deep cuts in my heart. "Isn't that what this is all about? Getting information enough on the AI to make better plans?"

"Liz got hurt by the biogear failing. You almost got killed. What happens if that happens, Lib? You're the only one who can make it. You're the only one who knows how to connect the way you to. You scare the clan, Lib. You know things no one else knows."

My throat tightens. Wolf's eyes seem to pin me to the spot. I do know things. I am different. I am clan now, but I am also something more. And I am not even certain what it is.

Why do I know how to rework gear? Why can I read code and hack into the AI's systems and manipulate the code lines? The AI—Conie—there are ties between us. At one time, I thought she was my mother. I no longer think that, but I cannot deny that Conie has a connection to me that leaves me uneasy.

I don't know what Wolf sees on my face, but he puts a hand on my shoulder as he did with Bird. I do not shake off his touch. He squeezes once, turns and walks away, heading down the tunnel, back to the main eating room.

Tension hunches his broad shoulders.

That did not go well—but I am still left with a job. I have gear to review and biogear to construct, and my old biogear to take apart to see why it, and Lizard's biogear, stopped working.

Chapter Three

Weaving through the new tunnels—and losing my way twice—I still manage to avoid running into anyone else.

This space wasn't part of the clan's old dwelling, but I asked Wolf for a corner in the new tunnels. I got it, but not much is here. Yellow light from the glowing parts of the drones brightens the room, as does the oil in the stone jars. We use these for lamps now in the Gear Room. I remembered how to make these after I found one in the Empties. But the rest of the clan still prefers to drill holes through the rock for light. Part of the biogear is making stronger drills for the clan, and no one seems to mind using that gear. But many avoid this place.

Even with the light, the workspace seems dim—and cluttered, the floor only dirt and piles of drone parts stacked in corners. Salvaged straight boards taken from the Empties give me a place to work on the gear.

Taking apart the drones gives my hands something to do and lets me forget about other things. I keep extra skins in the Gear Room so I can clean the parts and wipe off the organic bits of the drones. I can't do anything with the odd smell—like something died here. My thoughts circle back to the same place they always go. Soon, the AI will make her move. We have to stop her—*Conie*. That is my purpose now.

I try not to think of her. She scares and confuses me. There's an image I attach to her though—a woman with dark hair pulled back and a round, sweet face. She uses that face, but where did she find it? And why that face? Does she know that image draws me in and calms me? Is it the face of someone who was once alive?

I don't know—but I do want to find out.

That need drives me now as I was once driven to find the Glitches. Conie gave me that purpose, and sometimes words whisper in my head like memories. They are all that is left of the program put into me by the AI. It worries me that perhaps there is more still inside me that the AI can use.

I lay the gear out from the drones on the board I use to make biogear—wire, power-source box, circuits and a few components that I don't recognize. The drones have something organic-like inside—a brain of some kind that is tissue and fluid that acts like blood. They also have weapons—I have had these pointed at me too many times not to know what they look like. I will have to be careful with those.

There is always the chance that the AI might put traps in the drones, but I am not really sure she values this gear the way we do. The AI seems to only value the Norm—she seems willing to do anything to keep the Norm intact, and I don't know why she thinks that dome over a bunch of buildings is so important.

Staring at the pieces of the drone, now cleaned, it seems as if I am like this at times. Parts that don't connect—scattered memories that I still don't know if they are real. And I want to be real. I want…I want family, not just clan.

If I find my family, surely they'll want me and love me.

But is that true?

What if the AI—if Conie—really is my mother?

Lifting a hand, I stare at it. I scraped my knuckles and they are still bloody. My back still stings. Conie can't be my mother if I am real and she is only a construct, a computer program gone wrong. But the drones have something like blood and biological parts, and when I was inside the Norm I learned about something called a cyborg. Maybe I'm part machine somewhere inside?

I don't like that idea.

Letting out a breath, I start to organize the gear. I still don't know why acceptance is important to me. Maybe it has to do with having had my memories wiped, or having been put outside the Norm and used. Maybe that's created a drive in me to find the family I had before.

If they are still alive.

Which leads me back to thinking about Raj.

He was with the clan when I first arrived. He was a Glitch. He just wanted to go back to the Norm. He thought we could fix the AI. But it all went wrong. Some nights I dream of his dark brown eyes. His mouth opens and closes as if he is talking to me, but I hear no words.

"Get anything good today?"

The question makes me drop a coil of wire. I glance around. Alis stands next to me. She is one of the newer Glitches to have joined the clan, and she still has the pale skin of someone recently kicked out of the Norm. We are all clan now, but it does help to have someone who once was a Tech work with me on the biogear—Alis doesn't have the distrust of gear that Rogues have.

She leans forward to look over my shoulder. I think she is a little older than me, with big green eyes and long thick hair that's a shade of red I haven't seen on anyone else. Freckles dot her pale skin. Every time we go outside, her skin reddens into a burn. My own skin is now almost as dark as Bird's.

"I hope so. Three were hurt today."

She continues to stare at the gear. Her hair is pulled up and held together by two smoothed, polished sticks. It makes her look cute in a messy way. Reaching up, I brush a hand through my short hair. It never seems to grow.

Alis touches a finger to the power-source box. "Looks like it was worth the trip—and the injuries. I'd call this a success."

Something inside me eases. "That's what I thought." I pull the new, unknown gear away from her hands. "But we have to be careful. I don't want to trigger any hidden tracking devices."

She snorts but pulls her hands away. "You think the AI could do that? Would do that? Seems...I don't know, out of her focus on the Norm."

"She's an AI—Conie learns. Never forget that. Now help me clean up the scrap. We may be able to use some of the shells, but a lot of this is just junk."

We soon have everything organized—copper wires in spools, pieces of curved metal in one pile, flat metals in another, the outer shells of the drones stacked. The dead motherboards are useless, but I have four crystals that are new to me, and other circuits carefully put out of reach that I can study later. The rest will be given to the clan to use as decoration, or to make water bowls or maybe use as parts in the ATs.

Raj would have loved this.

I allow myself one, wistful wish that he was here. My heart tightens. Turning from the gear, I ask Alis, "Have you been making progress?"

She nods and gives me an eager smile. "Absolutely!" Moving to a stack of biogear in the corner, she lifts up one unit. Like all the others, it looks like a black turtle—one part flat and one part rounded. Wires with pointed tips extend out from the top to allow links into the skin. The biogear is designed to clamp onto the back and neck, and then extend out a visual screen for the wearer. I notice that Alis' biogear has the new extensions that come down the legs and also now has extensions that look as if they are meant to go along the wearer's arms. "I've improved the augments—this now increases upper body strength by nearly thirty percent. I smashed a rock with it."

"What about power usage?"

She frowns. "Well, it went down, but jumped up about thirty percent when I activated the arms."

"That's okay. We can work on it. But first, I need to figure out something else—we have a connection problem." I explain how my biogear shut down and disconnected—as did Lizard's.

Alis grimaces. "You think they ran out of power?"

I shrug. "That or maybe the drones sent a shutdown command. We need to figure it out. If someone's in the middle of jumping a canyon with biogear and it goes out, then—"

"Splat. Not fun. Maybe Dat can help."

I nod. Dat is even newer to the clan than Alis. He was half dead when Wolf and a small party had gone out to get water. He's almost fully recovered from that—but he's small and nervous and tends to be hard to find. He's also incredibly intelligent. A lot of the progress made on the biogear is because of his insights.

Dat is almost as smart as Raj, but his looks are opposite, with golden hair that is curling now he has enough water and food, pale skin, and eyes a honey brown with almost invisible eyelashes.

Raj would have liked Dat.

I squash the thought. It is too much of a distraction. But I am thinking more and more about Raj.

"Can I take a look at your biogear?" Alis asks. "Let's try a reboot."

I tell her I tried that already—twice. The biogear won't boot up again. Maybe I took out too many organic parts. But if a shutdown code was used, I will find it. Once I do, I will know how to reverse it and copy it. What worries me more is that I know these things without ever remembering how I learned them.

There isn't any explanation for how I am able to integrate gear off drones with my body—and with others. I just know how to do this. It is like breathing, something I do without really thinking about it.

Picking up my biogear, I stroke the smooth, round back. At times, it almost seems more a part of me than my own skin. The spots where it attaches with wires sharp as cactus needles no longer itch as they once did—in fact, I miss the wires when they are out.

Reluctantly, I hand the biogear to Alis. I pick up Lizard's biogear and we start to do a comparison.

Making the first biogear was almost more of an accident. I had no choice but to fight the AI outside the Norm—and found out drones could be brought down, that they were partly organic, and we could use that to make connections between our bodies and the gear. But the work is coming along too slowly—I only have four biogear sets. Four. And now two of them don't work.

We lay out the biogear, spreading wide the straps that create a sort of cage across the wearer's body. Two of the straps cross the belly and two cross the chest. Copper wiring lines every strap and wires attach to run points. Croc helped me figure this out—he knows every artery, every point where the nerves bunch. The wires allow power to be sent to the body to increase power and speed. Two wires hook into the neck, directly into the spine. In part, the biogear works off the wearer's own physical power—or that's how it's supposed to work.

As far as I can tell, the biogear works differently on me. It takes power from me, but it doesn't do that for others. And I can find no reason now why the biogear shutdown earlier. Everything should work.

Alis smooths a strap. "This is still the best piece of work I've seen, and you didn't even have as many materials as we have now. It's really incredible." She's looking at me the way she does sometimes. Like I'm better than anyone else in the clan. I shift and rub the back of my neck. Some part of me warms at her appreciation, but another part worries. I don't want to be better than, I want to be a part of something.

Reaching out, I touch one of the new pieces of gear that I don't recognize. I find a small depression and run my finger over it. A prick stings my finger and suddenly images fill my mind.

People fight over food—over water. They look gray and diseased, their skin mottled with sores, their clothes hanging in rags. The end of times…. Others call it a cleansing.

Knowledge rolls through my mind. *We failed in the last days of our world when we might have still been able to save it.*

Jerking my hand away, I break the link. I push away the gear. Did the AI want me to find this, or is this information all the drones have? Is it some little sliver of true history? Blinking, I turn to see that Alis hasn't even noticed anything—she studies the biogear as if puzzling out the answers, a small line between her eyebrows.

"Maybe it was just a loose connection? You know, if we use a better crystal—maybe the clear one you can't break —we could enhance the power capacities of the power-supply box and modify the motherboard to create a back-up. That way if there's a shutdown of the main power, the backup kicks in."

"Unless it's a full system shutdown." Alis' words trigger an idea. An ancient memory teases me, but I cannot quite pull it from hiding. I think to the images that flooded my mind a moment ago—war, battles, weapons that stopped things from working. Do such things still exist? And if they do, should I even consider trying to find such things?

I let the memory fade. I will hunt for it later. For now, Alis' idea is worth exploring.

I pull apart Lizard's biogear, working half absently. And I wonder if Wolf will ever wear the biogear. We are going to start to add weapons. It could mean the difference between life and death for us. But if Wolf will not adapt, is he going to end up hurt? Killed? The AI has drones, scabs…and sentinels within its artificial world. And maybe even things more dangerous. Conie knows we plan to fight her, so she has even more reason to want the clans gone. The clans steal water and resources from the Norm—resources the Norm needs if it is to leave this world and go to another one.

I grit my teeth against the thought—the AI doesn't have to destroy everything. Why does she think she must?

A ripple of dread races through me, lingering on my skin. I do not want this war to hurt anyone, but it will. And what if it takes Wolf from me? My heart slams into my ribs and my breath catches in my throat. I shudder.

"Lib? *Lib.*"

Looking up I see Alis staring at me with an expectant look on her face and her head tipped to one side. "I was asking if you think we need to try these new power-source boxes?" She breaks off, straightens and asks, "Want to tell me what's bothering you?"

"Why does something have to be brothering me?"

She shrugs, but her gaze sharpens. "You seem… distracted."

I bite my lip. I'm a little surprised by her perceptiveness. "Just…things on my mind."

The image flashes of the smooth corridors of the Norm. But this is not like earlier—this is a memory of how simple the Norm can seem. In some ways I understand why Raj thought to go back—he thought he could change the AI, make the Norm safe for everyone. And he, too, wanted to find his family.

Turning back to the biogear, I start to pull the power-supply box. "I'm just…it's just…well, I spoke with Wolf today and it didn't really end all that great." I push the hair from my forehead.

Alis nods. "Ah, I see. Male problems. I should have guessed. You're all moody. Can't think straight. That's what hanging around males does to you—makes you crazy." Leaning closer, she drops her voice slightly and asks, "You and Wolf…you ever find a quiet tunnel for getting together?"

I frown at her. I know this is the way of the clan. If a female is interested in a male, and he is interested as well, they can bond—they stand before the clan and swear an alliance to each other. But more often, males and females simply go off together when they want to. No one thinks anything about it. Very rarely, a baby will come of the coupling—but not often.

And I have never gone off with Wolf—except to train.

Except for that time he kissed me, making his interest known. But he has not kissed me since—and I don't know what I feel for him. Other than that I don't want to lose him from my side.

Staring at Alis, I wonder what I should tell her—or has she guessed everything and is just giving me a chance to talk. If she has noticed, others will have, too. After a moment, I ask, "Why do you think he would go with me?"

Turning back to the biogear, she straightens a wire. "Intuition. Plus, you seem to care what he thinks. I don't see anyone else having any sway over you, but you listen to him. So I figured there was something going on."

Heat stings my cheeks. I touch my fingers to them to cool the skin. "I do listen. But I don't go with him. He…I don't know if I want that complication."

She glances at me, one eyebrow quirks high. "Oh? Is that what's upsetting you? Not knowing?"

"I'm not upset about any of this." I slap the old power-supply box onto the wood, rattling other gear.

"You sure? In the Norm, I remember some saying how it used to happen so often that the AI started to assign partners. You know…set you up based on compatibility. The old stories say half the fighting in the Norm stopped." She lifts one shoulder. "But maybe that's just because the AI changed any Tech making trouble into a Glitch and dumped them. She changes whatever she can and gets rid of whatever she can't."

"I've never really thought of the AI in those terms—but it's true. I saw…Conie…the AI, manipulating and controlling the Tech in the Norm. She made them attack me and…well, a friend of mine. And then she just as easily made them stop. She changed their behavior to suit her will."

Alis winkles her nose. "Yeah, that's about what happened the day I was changed from Tech to Glitch—one day I'm doing my job, and one mistake later, I'm out of the Norm and thinking I'll die." She shivers. "I don't like to think about it."

Leaning my palms on the wood, I know what she means. It is difficult to recall memories of hard times. It is even more difficult to consider my feelings. They seem knotted in my stomach, tangled like crossed wires. Is Wolf the reason for this? Or is it just the entire day—the injuries and Bird and...

"I don't know what he feels." The words tumble out in a rush. "And that leaves me not knowing what I feel."

Alis turns to me and taps a finger on her lips. She narrows her eyes and then tells me, "I wouldn't worry about what he's feeling. He may be the leader of the clan, but you're the one who's going to lead us to a future where we're all still alive." Her voice is firm, even fierce, and her green eyes flash. "You need someone as progressive and strong as you are. You need someone who isn't afraid of biogear. That's our future."

Bracing one hand on the wood, I tell her, "Wolf is the leader—and clan law is that we follow. And he's the reason I'm as strong as I am. I wouldn't have made it without him. He trained me."

Alis slants a glance at me. "Maybe you need to consider the possibility that he's taught you all that he can. Maybe it's time to move on."

Her words leave my face cold and my heart pounding. I turn and leave, walking without really seeing where I am going. Is she right? I don't know, but I have to consider what she has said. And I am not really sure I want to.

Chapter Four

Working on the biogear with Alis and Dat keeps me busy. We add weapons to my gear and to Lizard's—and we upgrade the power supply boxes. This gives me an excuse to avoid Wolf, and he seems to have other worries, too. I see him during meal times, but he eats fast and leaves quickly. Skye does the same thing, which leaves me unhappy.

Skye was the first person I met after the AI put me outside the Norm. But I know she misses Raj as much as I do—maybe more. It seems to me that her eyes—once so blue—are pale now, and her hair seems more silver now than yellow like sunlight.

I don't know what to do to help her—should I talk about Raj to her or not? I do know she spends more time now with Bird, and less time with me. That is her choice.

Fixing the biogear is frustration. I have no answers for why it shut down, but at least the upgrades are going well. As I work, I try to focus on plans for what comes next. Not just ideas for getting water or food, which we have to do just to stay alive, but a bigger plan. We need to know AI's schedule for what she intends.

Imperfection constantly burdens humanity, but that can be remedied. In the end, the survival of humanity is all that matters.

That's what Conie told me when Raj and I managed to get into the Norm. But Conie views humanity as only the Techs she controls inside the Norm's dome. The Rogues—those born in the Outside—and the Glitches, the Techs Conie tosses out to recycle, meaning die, don't matter to her. They just consume resources.

Wolf teaches me that the Outside has life—cactus and other plants that hold water, and animals we can track and eat. But resources are scarce—the AI hordes them. I worry, too, that the AI may be trying to kill us by using up all the resources. Or keeping them from us somehow.

But none of that matters if the AI leaves, gouging out a huge chunk of the world to separate the Norm from the earth.

This knowledge leaves me shaking inside. It is even possible to stop the AI? Or change her? Raj thought we could, and I worry that he is dead now because of such hopes. Which leads me back to needing the biogear—I need to hack the AI, and for that I need a better connection. The AI has been slowly increasing security along all the places we used to use for connects—now they are guarded by drones in the Outside and firewall sentinels in the AI's artificial world. So I need to figure out how the AI—how Conie—talks to the drones. If I can work that out, I can work a connect back to her. And maybe we'll have a chance.

I'm staring at the new gear from the drones when a soft step behind me startles and makes me turn. Wolf stands in the rough entrance to the Gear Room, his shoulders almost touching the sides of the tunnel. I let out a breath.

"Better?" he asks.

I'm not sure if he means am I feeling better or am I doing better at getting the biogear to work, or is it working better. With a shrug, I pick up a power-supply box. "Take this—it'll work in an AT. Hook it up to charge from the solar panels."

Coming over, Wolf takes the slim, black box and our fingers brush.

Turning away, I ask, my voice a little rough, "Do you… ever regret having taken me in?"

The muscles in his jaw twitch. "Everyone matters, Lib. You know that. I have to protect everyone."

I frown and look away. "We are protecting them." Glancing at him, I ask, "Don't you trust me? Do you think —I told you I'm not really a Glitch…I'm something else. The AI sent me here to find you—to help her eliminate you, but I didn't. Doesn't that count? Or do you think the AI is still using me? Is that why everyone thinks bringing gear in is bad—it's too much of the AI here where we live?"

Everything in his body seems to ease slightly. He reaches out, touches his fingers to my shoulder and slides his touch down the length of my bare arm until he can wrap his hand around my wrist. I take a quick, deep breath, but don't pull away. His voice softens. "I trust you. But I worry." Letting go of me, he waves at the gear. "This—it's dangerous. Last time out, we could have lost you."

My heart thumps so loud it feels like a drumbeat echoing in the tunnels. My skin tingles where Wolf touched me, and the sound of his soft, deep voice washes over me in a way that's both soothing and electrifying. I step closer to him. I want to wrap myself in his arms and let the rest of the world fade away.

He reaches up and his hand hovers just above my cheek. Shifting, he smooths my hair and rests his palm against the side of my face. I'm left breathless. I tilt my head back so I can look into his eyes. It's too dark in the Gear Room to see colors—his face is shadows and stark lines—but I can see the warmth in his eyes. And something more.

"Lib." He breathes out my name with a whisper and leans toward me. I take in a breath to fill my senses with how he smells—like earth and sky and wind. Wolf always smells good to me.

Anticipation tingles on my skin and sweeps into me with a fire like the sparking power from the biogear. "Wolf?"

The word echoes down the tunnel and into the Gear Room. Wolf's hand drops from my face and he straightens.

Now my mouth twitches down and I turn to the entrance to see who robbed me of Wolf's kiss.

Otter, who is dark skinned and older than Wolf, stops at the entrance to the Gear Room. He glances around as if he doesn't trust anything in here. "You said come find you when the others are ready. Got 'em rounded up for a water hunt."

Wolf nods. He glances at me, touches the back of my hand with one finger, and says, "We got along before this stuff. We can figure out how to fight without it, too."

He leads Otter away. I watch them go. Turning back to the gear, I see that Wolf left the power-supply box.

He may trust me—but he doesn't trust the biogear. And now I know that he has no idea how powerful the AI really is. Our paths are starting to go in separate directions, and that leaves me rubbing my arms and feeling cold inside.

*   *   *

Hunger drives me from the Gear Room at last—and thirst. I have my biogear working again, and Lizard's too. An idea for how to wire in the new power source packs worked, and I bring them and one more with me to the main room.

The rest of the clan has already eaten, and many are getting ready to head out. Night is a dangerous time to hunt, but it is cool at night and the night predators hunt for small game, not large packs. We have safety in numbers. I drink a flask of water and eat some dried meat, then it is time to slip on my biogear. It goes on like a second skin, with only a small prick of the wire needles. Even though I have adapted the biogear to include weapons from two of the drones we downed, I still tuck Raj's knife into my belt. It is mine now. And a reminder that even good plans can turn to dust.

Wolf gives orders for who will go out on what teams.

Skye eyes the biogear, but when I hold one out to her she shakes her head. Mostly, I think she's afraid—she hates connecting with the AI, even for something as simple as opening a water pipe. Maybe she's right. She's had trouble with connects before. Maybe the biogear would be bad for her. But Wolf says she is to go with me.

I think about how he said he worries for me.

I keep thinking of him, how he held my hand, and touched my cheek.

The thoughts distract me, so I shake them up and focus on hooking Lizard into her biogear. Tiger steps forward to take up his biogear. Tiger is one of the youngest Rogues—he's skinny and small, but he is as fierce as Wolf and never lets his size stop him from doing anything.

After I have Tiger's biogear fastened on him, Bird comes into the main room, handing out skins of water to take with us. She glances at the biogear on Tiger and her face pales then reddens. When she looks at me, her eyes seem accusing, as if somehow I forced the biogear onto Tiger.

Bird turns away, but Wolf steps in front of her, forcing her to stop. "You're staying." He sounds weary, as if he's told Bird this before.

"Lizard's going. I want to go." She lifts her chin. She still wears cloth wrapped around the arm that was burned. "I don't like sitting around doing nothing."

"Has Croc cleared you?"

Bird looks away. She's shorter than Wolf and with her back turned, I can't see her expression, but I wonder if she is going to tell the truth or not. She tugs at one of the ribbons woven into her hair and after a moment says, "The burn's almost healed. Going out tonight isn't going to be a problem. And...and I just have a feeling you need me."

Wolf rubs at his cheek. Golden stubble dots his chin and face—he usually shaves it off with his knife but he has not done that today. Is he searching for a way to tell her no without sounding mean about it?

Glancing around, I know the other two teams are full. If Bird goes, she will have to head out with my group. I don't want that. Bird doesn't like the biogear and I worry she will do everything she can to make it seem that the biogear isn't working right.

I know she's only doing what she thinks is right, but that still doesn't make it a good idea to send her out.

For a brief moment, I wonder if I should get Wolf to swap her into another team and I could take someone else with me. But this is Wolf's call to make. I can't...I won't have others thinking I am trying to undermine his leadership.

Wolf shakes his head and tells Bird, "There will be other missions."

"You used to listen to me when I said I had a bad feeling. I need to go. I have to be out there."

I want to ask why—what is she worried about? The biogear failing again? Or something else? But Wolf has already made up his mind. I see it in his eyes, in the short nod he gives.

My throat tightens and my fingers chill.

Wolf looks at me over the top of Bird's head. His gaze is intense and uncertain, as if he is trying to tell me something with just a look. What—does he want me to understand? To look after Bird for him?

I look away, but Wolf calls out, "Bird's going with you, Lib." He turns and walks away with the group he is leading on the scavenge.

Bird walks over to me and stops in front of me. She waves a hand at me, not quite slapping the biogear, as if she can't bring herself to touch it. "You really sure you got this working right?"

*   *   *

Our group is scavenging water. Wolf and another group head out on a scavenge for food—plants and meat. I hate the water scavenges—they're getting harder and harder. The AI knows we need water and is making it harder for us to get a connect and hack into water storage. Conie seems to want to hoard every resource that exists. That makes me think she is planning to leave sooner than we know.

The sun is dropping quickly behind hills and the orange glow makes the Outside look as though it's on fire. Pretty, I suppose. I have Bird, Lizard, Tiger, Skye, Otter and Otter's brother, Sidewinder, with me. Everyone knows what to do —that we have to be quiet and we have to move fast. Lizard and I can move faster with biogear so we scout ahead. The screen on the biogear helps with spotting drones, but it doesn't help if the drone has landed, shutdown its system and is in hiding.

As the sun goes down, the danger goes up. I hear whispers behind me.

"Bird has a bad feeling so maybe we shouldn't be out tonight." The voice—low and rough—sounds like Sidewinder.

Otter's snort and low laugh is unmistakable. "So we sit and cower—and go thirsty. Relax. We've got an advantage."

"What? Gear off some drone? It failed last time out."

Walking faster, I move ahead of the group. I have no interest in their worries.

Bird Sees Far does see things—I know this. Everyone listens when she tells of her dreams. I don't know how she knows this—I just know that not everything she sees comes true. It is as if she can see possibilities at times. I don't understand it. It's not like when I connect—I see things then but what I see is into the AI's artificial world. And my dreams are more about elusive memories. Or that's what I hope—because my dreams are not always good ones.

The world around us turns purple overhead and a chill wind springs up.

I am trying to help, I remind myself. What we're doing is important, and that's enough right now to spur me forward.

We head to a station not far from the Norm. I expect to see drones, but I am hoping not very many will be at this station. We hit this station for water not that long ago, so the AI may not expect us to hit it again. The ground under my boots is dry and dusty. The biogear lets me see more than anyone—I glimpse heat from the bodies of smaller animals as they scurry away, and from larger ones who watch us as we pass.

To keep the new tunnels hidden, we take the long way to the station, through a narrow canyon and up over a high ridge. The biogear seems to be working perfectly, helping me walk fast and without effort, letting me see into the night almost as if it was daylight still.

Skye jogs up beside me. For a minute, we walk in silence, and then Skye says, "Bird seems a little irritated lately."

I shrug. "Not much fun to get hurt." And she didn't see that coming—did that upset her?

The last of the sun's light is gone. A few stars appear in the black sky and a sliver of a moon is rising. This would be a faster run with ATs, but Wolf took the three out that we have. Our goal is to hit the station, connect, and send water to a pickup spot that is some distance from the Norm. That is the goal, anyway. If we're lucky, we'll succeed. Not so lucky means maybe we can get a little water—Otter and Sidewinder have skin bags just in case we only can tap into water at the station. At the worst, we won't get anything, but I don't intend for that to happen.

Skye glances at me and says, a little breathless from having to walk fast to keep up with me, "Do you remember Chandra? And Marq? Seems like no one even notices that they're gone."

I wet my lips—Skye left out one name. Raj. We were once all Glitches in the clan—myself, Skye, Raj, Chandra, Marq. My chest tightens. I don't want to keep losing people, but what choice do we have?

I risk a quick look at her. She is looking down at the dirt and her boots. Her blonde hair slides forward over one shoulder so I can't really see much of her expression, but her voice carries a bitterness I haven't heard from her before.

Shaking my head, I ask, "What were we supposed to feel?"

Skye looks up at me. Her mouth thins and she hunches a shoulder. "Is that you talking or the biogear? Maybe Bird's right—maybe it's not giving you as much as it's taking out of you."

I don't know what to say to this. Skye slows and falls back, but the biogear's screen shows me the square of the station on the horizon. It's a flat metal platform, with four posts, a metal roof and a connect railing inside the station. Three walls provide shelter from the dust that can rage across the Outside. The fourth wall is just glass that will slide to one side at a touch.

I wave for the others to hurry and we all break into a jog.

At the station, I scan the sky. No drones so far. Pointing to the left of the station and the railing where Skye will try for a connect, I tell the others, "Otter, Tiger and Sidewinder head up on that outcropping of rocks. Lizard keeps watch.

Bird—stay close and watch Skye's back. I'll stick with Skye in case the connect goes bad and she hits any firewall sentinels."

Bird stares at me for a long time, her eyes narrowed. I don't know if she's unhappy that I'm giving orders or if her bad feeling about this scavenge has gone to worse. Her stare leaves me uneasy, feeling as if I have overlooked something, but I can't think what.

Skye and I start moving to the station and the railing that allows a connect to the AI…or at least to the part of the AI programming that siphons water from the Outside, from underground springs and rivers. I glance back at Bird. She is still staring at me, as if I've already done something terrible—something unforgivable.

So I ask, "Bird?"

Bird clenches and unclenches one fist. Her eyes are bright and glittering, seeming to catch every glint of starlight. The wind flutters the ribbons braided into her hair. This is not the time or place to have anything out, and I open my mouth to tell Bird that. But she turns away.

I let out a whoosh of air I didn't realize I was holding. Turning away from Bird, I head over to stand next to Skye within the station.

Skye rubs her palms against her thighs. "I wish you guys weren't fighting," she tells me in a small voice. She doesn't look at me.

"It's not a fight. And we're all clan now." Or that's what I hope.

"Maybe," Skye says.

Glancing around, I use the biogear screen to check the area. Still no drones. Now I'm uneasy, but I don't know if that's from the lack of drones on guard or Bird acting oddly.

I wait until Otter and Sidewinder wave to me from the rocks, Lizard is walking around the station and looks as nervous as I am. Tiger has all but disappeared beside the trunk of a half-dead tree near Otter. It's an impressive feat, but there is none better at hiding than Tiger. Bird settles herself at the edge of the station, making sure her boots are not on the metal platform and pointedly not looking at either me or Lizard.

Turning to Skye, I ask, "Are you ready?" I wish Skye wasn't here. I want it just to be me, making the connect, risking an encounter with the AI or with her firewall sentinels inside her artificial construct. I worry that someday Skye won't get out of a connect. That she'll get stuck—just like Raj got caught somehow in the Norm. I will never tell her any of this.

She looks up at me and smiles, but it's a shadow of the energy she once had. She's not quite the same anymore—not since Raj. "Let's go." She puts her hand on the railing, and I see her eyes go distant as she slips into the connect.

I wait for a moment, giving her time to settle. Putting my hand on the railing, I wait.

Connection: secure.

Familiar pinpricks sting my palm. I close my eyes. When I open them a second later, I am in the familiar virtual world of the AI.

Around me appears a room with no walls and soft, blue lighting. I have been here before. On either side of me filing cabinets rise up like tall canyon walls, representations of where things are kept by the AI. Of course, they're virtual like everything else. I am even more worried now. Normally, a sentinel would have appeared—a firewall to block access. Why haven't we seen one yet?

"Should we look for water?" Skye asks with a waver in her voice as if she has never done this before.

I nod. "Water and if you find seeds, we should take them, too."

"I'll start down there." She points along the seemingly endless row of filing cabinets to our left. Turning, she begins walking, scanning the cabinets, her fingers plucking at the hem of her skin shirt.

To the right, a screen appears. This has happened before, too. I must be careful of my thoughts. The biogear makes my connect even stronger—I can manipulate this world with the biogear, I can make things appear as I wish. And I was not careful just now—I let the questions in my mind wander, and the screen appeared for me.

I cannot resist such a perfect opportunity.

My palms itch. This is dangerous and not strictly part of the mission. But this is access, and we need to know more.

Heading to the screen, I put my fingertip on it and begin to search. Lists flash over the screen, whirring numbers, lines of code. With the biogear I can scan more rapidly than ever before. It takes me a moment before I stop at lines of code that shift into words. Into information.

On me.

Lib aged to approximately sixteen physical years. Learning capabilities evolved at an increased rate as have complex thoughts. Human faults appearing. These may result in difficulties with completing the program. Suggested solution: memory wipe. Will result in inherent desire to return to the system.

There is more. Statistics on my growth and education. Knowledge of a world that no longer exists is hidden somewhere within my memory—or was that wiped, too?

Suddenly, flashes, images explode in my mind. The Empties....but not the Empties...looking lush and glittering, not twisted and crumbling. I pull away from the screen, but the connection seems to have jarred something lose inside my head. Why is the AI—why is Conie—so focused on me?

Lifting my hand to my chest, I curl my fingers tight. This wasn't what I wanted. I haven't found anything on the AI. And there's nothing here about my parents. Nothing to tell me who I really am.

Nothing to help me stop the AI.

Turning, I try to calm my spinning thoughts, to focus them and bring up information on the AI's plans. I intend to keep searching for answers.

A scream shatters that idea.

Running down between the cabinets, I shout, "Skye!"

She screams again, and I find her slumped to her knees, trembling and jerking uncontrollably. Is she having a seizure? She was thrown out of the Norm, made a Glitch because of this seizing activity, but then I glimpse the sentinel.

Skye is slumped over the sentinel firewall, and the black thing is sparking. I know this is a construct—it is an artificial world. But the firewall can still kill. It's connected to Skye's mind, and is trying to shut down her brain.

The biogear lets me move fast and I'm stronger—even in this artificial world, the biogear gives me an edge. I grab the sentinel and drag it out from under Skye's body. Energy pulses through me, waves of shocks. For a moment everything goes black, and I slip into a deeper connect.

I don't know this place. It seems cold and unnatural. And I am not alone.

Conie seems to step from the darkness—she takes form, but she is only a projection. And she still wears the face I know, the one that I think she took from my mother. My throat seems to stop working and a band tightens around my chest. That face seems kind—an oval shape with a chin that tapers to a point and high cheekbones and soft skin. But her eyes are wrong. They glow impossibly blue, lit by power.

She reaches for me with long, delicate fingers. Her nails seem like pretty half-moons. So much attention for something that isn't real.

Heat dances across my skin like tiny particles of sand jumping along my arms. I want to step back, to turn away. I want to leave, but I cannot.

Her voice slips into my head—it's the connect, I know. She has dragged me here, and now Conie speaks to me.

It's an advantage. The same advantage that presented itself when I decided on a Glitch in the first place. You would be taken in. You would be accepted. A drone could never do that. They are too random—but you were specific. You were to be a force that would trap them all. Now you are my biggest failure. Failures must be eliminated.

Electricity slams into me, seems to wrap around my heart and my mind.

Once the AI wanted me to survive. That time is gone.

But Conie doesn't know the biogear has changed me.

Power surges into me, but I direct it into the biogear, channeling it, using it. Slowly I shift it. Conie's face blanks, then wavers and vanishes. I am in the black room but all I need to do is think of Skye and in the next instant I stand over her, back between the row of filing cabinets. The sentinel is still in my hands.

A buzzing seems to fill my mind. Energy gathers in my fingertips. I slam it into the sentinel. It makes a loud, skittering sound like tiny pellets hitting metal. Sparks seem to sizzle in the air. The whole construct of the virtual world seems momentarily to dim. And the sentinel firewall crumbles into nothing, becomes only flashes of codes, bits of ones and zeros.

I lean on Syke's slumped form, exhausted. Every muscle aches, and the spot where Conie touched me feels as if it has been burned.

Conie—that thought has me straightening. Conie will not rest—and she wants me dead. She wants all of us dead.

With a groan, I jerk upright and pull on Skye's arm. We have to leave the connect.

The thought breaks the connection.

In the next instant, I am Outside again, standing on the metal platform with Skye's real arm in my hands and a cold wind slapping my face and the night dark around us. The biogear is a comforting weight on my shoulders and I use the screen to scan Skye.

She lives. Ragged breaths lift her chest, and the biogear screen shows me a low body temperature and that she has not sustained damage. The encounter with the sentinel firewall has left her unconscious. Relief trickles through me and I kneel next to Skye.

Grabbing her shoulder, I shake her, just as I am shaking inside still from my encounter with Conie. "Skye, wake. You must wake. We have to go."

This is too much like the time when I first met Skye and a connect had gone bad. She doesn't respond. We've been here too long, and Conie is going to come after me. The last time Skye had a bad connect, it took hours for her to wake.

We don't have hours.

Maybe I can carry her—maybe the biogear makes me strong enough to do that.

A low whine fills the night. Drones. Looking up, I see five coming—the biogear screen shows them as bright flashes, moving fast. "Bird, in here—I need help with Skye. Everyone else, find cover—drones!" I yell the words, and drag Skye's limp body with me.

Where is Bird?

At the edge of the station, I turn and use the biogear screen to get a sight on one of the drones. A thought activates the beam of cohesive light—it shoots out from a point near my right shoulder, hits the drone and sends it spinning to the ground to land with a crash and a flash of light.

Turning, I scan for the others.

Otter launches himself from the rocks and onto one of the drones. The black drone wobbles and an arm lashes out, but Otter grabs it, swings down on it and snaps off the weapon arm. He hits the ground, tosses the weapon arm to Sidewinder, who turns and slams the arm into another drone as it sweeps down.

Lizard's scream tears the air. Turning, I see Lizard aiming at one drone, but another pins her to the ground with a metal arm through her back. Blood spurts. Lizard shoots at one drone. A hole appears in it and it falls into an oozing heap, the green goo sliding out of it. But Lizard is still pinned by the second drone.

In the next moment, I slam into the drone holding Lizard, it shatters, splashing goo over us. I slam a fist into it and pain explodes up my arm but the drone spirals away and smashes into a rock. My biogear leaves me strong enough to dent the drone, and I hit it with a blast from my weapon, dropping it dead. Yet another drone tries to grab my arm. Metal slices my skin, but I turn and slam a fist down on it. It lets got and skitters away.

Grabbing Lizard, I drag her with me. Her face is even paler than the moon, but she is breathing. Blood darkens the back of her skin tunic. "Move," I shout. My biogear screen shows two more drones coming for us.

There are more than I thought there would be. A lot more.

A drone closes on us. I get Lizard safe under a rock overhang and dart out. Unsheathing Raj's dagger, I plunge it into the drone in front of me, aiming for the joint between mental and the weapon arm it has aimed at someone. The black drone sparks, goo leaks out of it. It wobbles and falls to the ground.

Panting now, I stand and shout. "Everyone down. Get down. Now!"

Lifting my arm, I sight the next drone with the biogear screen. That's all I do for the next few breaths—for the next dozen heartbeats. Sight—fire. Sight—fire. The sky seems to brighten with the beams of light that lash the air, sizzling, leaving it smelling like metal and meat thrown onto a fire. Suddenly, I scan the sky and see nothing—no dots on the screen. No more drones. We have a breather.

A cry of rage echoes.

Bird launches herself up from the ground, a rock in her hands, its edge jagged. She lands on the smoking shell of a drone and strikes it hard. Lifting the rock, she slams it down again and again, splattering the ground with its green goo from the organics inside.

Sparks fly. The drone tries to lift a weapon arm, and Bird smashes that.

Heading over to her, I grab Bird's arm. "Enough. It's done." She tries to jerk away, but I hang onto her wrist. "If you keep doing that, we won't be able to get any parts from it!"

She freezes, the rock held above her head. She turns to look at me, her chest heaving and ribbons flying everywhere. Standing, she throws the rock down.

"Use it? Is that all you can think about?" She waves a hand around us. "You need better eyes. I told you—I told Wolf—I had a bad feeling. This is worse than bad."

A tingle spreads down my spine. My arm hurts. My head hurts. I would like nothing better than to sink onto the sand and collapse, but I look around, searching for the others..

A dark streak weaves down Tiger's face. He has pulled off his biogear and it looks like he has been using it more like a club to bash drones. But he stands defiant, legs spread wide, looking ready to keep fighting, a thick tree branch held in one hand. Skye is sitting up again, holding her head and leaning against one of the posts that hold up the station's roof. Lizard still lies under the rock overhang where I left her, but the biogear screen shows no heat from her, no heartbeat, no breathing.. She is dead—and I will forever miss her. Why did she have to try and take on two drones?

Turning away, I swallow bile.

There should be two more.

The biogear screen helps me to find them—but I see only one heat signature. I spot Otter first. His sandy hair is left pale by the thin moonlight. His body is still warm, still giving off heat, and he is bent over something. I walk closer and the something dark becomes a body— Sidewinder.

The blood turns black in the moonlight. Glancing around, I tell the others, "We didn't get water, so grab what you can from the drones we downed. They shouldn't have died for nothing."

Chapter Five

We make the trip home in silence. I bring Lizard's biogear. We can't bring the dead with us—the bodies are too heavy and the clan has no use for the dead. We strip the bodies of anything useful and leave the dead to the scavenger animals. Clan law is that nothing is wasted—not even the dead. Lizard and Sidewinder will give a meal to the animals who roam the Outside, just as the animals sometimes give meals to the clan.

When we get back to the tunnels, things will need to be said. The dead will be remembered around the meal fire—someone must speak of their lives and how they died. I am left feeling hollow.

Is this all useless?

It has to mean something.

I managed to get away from Conie—out of the connect she pulled me into. That has to be a sign that she can be defeated. Isn't it? Or am I fooling myself? Will I end up dead like the others? Will we all become so much dust?

I try not to think about their faces. Sidewinder had a crooked smile, and Lizard wore her biogear as if it was an honor. Knowing they're dead leaves my chest tight and my hands shaking. But I feel no urge to cry. Is that wrong?

And that leaves me thinking about what Skye said of Chandra and Marq. It makes me wonder if I shouldn't be crying.

We reach the tunnels long before daybreak, and thankfully without encountering more drones or anything else. The biogear is a help there—I can see the drones long before they reach us. I hear their whine. We have to hide twice to avoid them—but I am too tired to fight and I see the others staggering as we head to the tunnels.

There is always someone waiting for us in the tunnels when we return. Part of this is for security—you never know who might stumble into a tunnel entrance. The other part of this is in case we come back with injured—Croc is always one of those who waits for those returning from a scavenge.

Usually, I'm happy to see the shine on Croc's bald head, or to hear the soft questions of those who greet us. Tonight,

I want nothing more than a place to sleep. I know I won't be that lucky.

We come back without water. We come back leaving two behind.

I drop down into the tunnel behind Skye. I am the last to come in. From deeper in the tunnels, voices carry to me, one higher in pitch and the other rumbling. Bird and Wolf are arguing. Usually, it's about me.

Or maybe it's about the biogear.

With a sigh, I head their way. I don't even bother asking the others to take what little we salvaged to the Gear Room. And it is very little. We took down almost a dozen drones, but most of them ended up smashed or fell to the ground so far away we couldn't retrieve much.

The echo of Bird's voice reaches me now. "She wanted parts. She's more machine than anything else now. She didn't care that two died—just for more drone parts."

The words sting even, but a squirming in my gut makes me wonder if she isn't right. What if I am something Conie created? What if the biogear is changing me?

I can't cry—isn't that just how a machine would operate?

Reaching Bird and Wolf, I glance from one pale face to the other. Glowing rocks help illuminate this part of the tunnels—we have a few rocks that glow at night with an odd green color. Wolf looks grim, his forehead is lined and his dark eyes are unreadable. He stands with his arms folded across his chest. He doesn't even glance at me.

Bird shifts so her back is to me. "Otter's taking the loss pretty hard." Her voice is laced with stinging anger.

Wolf drops his hands to his side and then rubs one palm over his face. "What happened?"

Bird shoots me a glance, her back stiff and her face an odd color in the green light. "The connect took too long. I told you I had a bad feeling, but you didn't listen. She didn't listen. We shouldn't have gone out tonight—and that gear stuff didn't help Lizard. It—"

"Bird." The one word is sharp and Wolf lifts a hand. "Save it for council. For now, we remember those we lost."

My mouth dries, but I head over to Wolf. "It was no one's fault. "We couldn't have known it—"

"Save it," Wolf says. "You can speak at council."

*   *   *

Remembering those we have lost is never easy for me. I sit in the back of the main room, hungry but I can't bring myself to eat. I still have on my biogear and it seems a comfort to me.

Otter speaks for Sidewinder. I don't really understand the closeness that Otter and Sidewinder shared. I've never had a brother—not that I remember. Or a sister. When I try to recall being little, flashes of what almost seem like memories start to come to me only to blank out. I have no past—no childhood. I can envy the pride in Otter's voice as he speaks of him and Sidewinder going out on their first scavenge when they were still small. But I don't envy the pain in his voice as he speaks of Sidewinder's courage in his last moments.

It's time then to speak of Lizard, and several of the clan look to me. I stare back. What can I say? I didn't know

Lizard when she was young. Do they want me to talk of the biogear? How Lizard was brave enough to put it on and wear it? Or how she was foolish enough to try and fight two drones at once?

Glancing at Bird, I see her staring at me, her eyes hot, almost as hot as the fire in the center on the main room. The fire dances shadows over the walls, and I wonder if Lizard and Sidewinder's shadows are there, watching us. My throat tightens. I cannot say anything.

Wolf stands and talks of Lizard. I hear of how she was small and how Wolf taught Lizard to track. How Lizard got her name because she liked to crawl when she first came to this world and was slow to learn to walk. Wolf tells more stories of her, and I start to see that Lizard did not put on the biogear because she was brave—she put it on to compensate. She was small, she was slower than others, she wanted to do more—and the biogear made her stronger.

That was why she took on two drones—she had something to prove.

I am starting to see we don't need to train on how to use the biogear, we need more training on fighting with the biogear and finding its limitations.

Wolf's voice fades into silence. I glance up and see that the time to remember is over. Wolf stands over me. He sits down on the ground next to me. I stare at my hands, holding them in my lap.

Wolf asks, "Going to talk to me?"

I glance at him. "About what? What do you want?" He shakes his head. "You didn't speak for Lizard. That was cruel."

Leaning my back against the rough stone, I tell him, "You said things better than I would. You knew Lizard longer than I did."

He offers me a half smile. "I would speak for you, Lib. You're special and you're doing good work. You're part of the clan and you need to think more of the whole."

"You don't think I do?"

"We lose two. Then two more. And if that keeps happening, soon there is no clan. There is nothing. We cannot fight if we lose the clan. What's the point in that?"

I shake my head. "I know. But...I don't have the answers. This doesn't...this isn't what I wanted. I'm trying to do what's best for everyone, too."

He shrugs. "You're pushing, Lib. What happened in the connect?"

I turn away from him. "Does it matter? What happened is done."

"It is. But if we don't know why, it'll happen again. Until the council speaks, we stay inside—we stay safe. Understand?"

Stiffening, I shoot him a look. "How is that safe? We don't know when the AI is going to try to leave. We don't know anything."

He shakes his head. "Others dying isn't going to get us answers. Look around. Clan is small—we waste nothing and tonight was a waste." He stands. My throat is tight again and my pulse hammers. I know he's right, but hiding in the tunnels isn't going to keep us alive. He runs one hand through his hair. It's gotten shaggy and hangs down past his shoulders. "Come to council. You should speak."

Pressing my hands against my thighs, I hope they aren't shaking. The last time I was in front of the council, they were deciding on my fate and intent on throwing me out. Have I come back to the same place? "I don't want to."

After a moment, he says, "You need to be there. There are things only you can say. Things only you know. Be there, Lib. And leave off your gear."

Chapter Six

While Wolf is clan leader, the council makes the big decisions. If they decide I've done something wrong, they can decide to ban me from the clan. Banishment to the Outside is just about a death sentence, unless another clan takes me in.

The only other council meeting I have been to did not leave me with the best of feelings toward them.

Still wearing my biogear, I stand in the new council room, chin up and mouth pressed tight. This is just like the last council room, wide and with a low, rough ceiling dug out of soft rock, a sand floor, and a single hole in the ceiling that lets in moonlight right now.

Seven others of the clan sit in front of me on rocks dragged into the chamber from the Outside. The council is always older members of the clan—the youngest are Wolf and Bird. The council should be nine, but now it is only seven who sit in a semi-circle—the council has lost members before this, and will lose more in this war with the AI. I know this and shiver a little. The council room always seems cold.

Bird sits with the others, between Lion—who has never liked me and who stares at me now with ice in his eyes—and a man named Horse. Bird, who has been talking to Horse, breaks off her words and frowns at me. Wolf is here, sitting next to Wind, who is mother to Mouse and who comes to the Tracker Clan from another clan. Wind at least smiles at me with a kindly face. A woman named Elk, who spoke for me in the last council, gives me a nod.

The seventh in the council is a man I recognize. He has no hair but shaves his head with a knife blade. He also has eyes of a pale, golden color. He's only a few years older than Wolf and goes by the name of Komodo. I've never been on a scavenge with him, and I didn't know he was on the council. I don't even know how the council is chosen, but it seems odd to me that while Glitches are now part of the clan, there are only Rogues, only those born here in the Outside, on the council.

Trying to stand taller, I meet the stares of those who are seated. There are two extra stone seats, but I would rather stand and face everyone.

81

"Do you know why you are here?" Elk asks.

Everyone else stops talking. I dart a stare at Bird, but her expression is blank. Looking back at Elk, I tell her, "Not exactly."

Elk inclines her head and says, "Council is called because any loss is a hard one—and there is some thought that losses may come from the gear you have us taking."

"What?" I blurt out the word. Wolf shoots a hard stare at me and I swallow any more words. Komodo and Bird are frowning at me, and even Wind shakes her head, her long hair swaying as if she does not approve that I did not control myself. Only Lion rolls his eyes as if he expected me to not behave well.

Elk keeps talking, her voice even and calm. "We must question if the gear you bring—what you call biogear—brings more drones after us. Is it really a help to us, or is it a danger?" Her stare lingers on me, not unkindly, but as though to measure me from the inside out.

I swallow the anger simmering inside. How can they not see that the biogear is our only hope? We won a small battle with so very little, and the only thing that saved us was using the drone gear against the drones. We can't defeat the AI with rocks and knives.

Sucking in a breath, I part my lips to try and tell them some of this, but Wolf speaks first, his voice low and soft. "Some think the AI will never take the Norm away—that such a thing is impossible."

"Impossible?" I repeat. "Is that because I'm the only one who has spoken to the AI? They think I'm lying?"

Bird lifts her chin. "The AI lies all the time—doesn't she? Isn't that what you've told us?"

I have to nod. "She does lie. And maybe…just maybe it will be impossible for her to take the Norm away into space. Maybe it won't happen until the children of Mouse grow up…or the children of Mouse's children. But does anyone really think the AI doesn't want every Rogue and Glitch dead? Every clan wiped out? We take water from the AI…we steal resources she wants for the Norm. We've been in a war with the AI for a very long time. This has to end—or the AI will end all of us"

Bird takes a deep breath. When she speaks, I can tell she's making an effort to be reasonable. "Things are changing. Rapidly. Everyone understands that. But what if you're going about helping in the wrong way? Gear is doing more harm than good. It will destroy us."

"Will it? What about how the biogear saved almost everyone from that scavenge that went wrong? Lizard tried to fight two drones—that's why she died. Sidewinder didn't have biogear on—if he had, he might be alive still. I fought off almost a dozen drones because of my biogear. Are you saying we all should have just died there? That we need to throw away the biogear and hide in the tunnels and just hope the AI decides to stay?"

Bird shakes her head. "Maybe those drones found you because of the gear you had on. You keep talking about fighting with your biogear. That gear doesn't let you hide—which is what we used to do. That gear hasn't let you do anything to stop the AI."

"Biogear has made hunting easier—we can find food faster, can scavenge water with less risk."

Komodo frowns. "Easier does not mean they are *better*. The words are not the same. And we had far less trouble with the AI before you started attacking the drones. Why do you take clan out to die?"

I open my mouth to argue, but Elk holds up her hand. "The council meets to talk about life. We must look to how we can avoid the clan dying because too many die."

Glancing around the faces turned toward me, I ask, "Don't you see—this is what the AI wants. All the clans hiding and afraid to come out—afraid of trying to stop her plans. If you don't fight, we'll all die. How is that going to save you?"

Bird's shoulders sag. For a second, her expression softens and she looks almost sympathetic. "So we must sacrifice the one to save the many?"

"Yes. Because there won't be a single one of us left if we don't. This is a war and the AI will do anything to win it."

Bird nods. "According to you."

My heart thuds into my chest. If Raj were here, he could tell them about the AI. But he's not here. It is only my word that the AI has terrible plans for this world. I glance around the room, trying to see who believes in me and who doesn't. I see only doubt and uncertainty.

"Yes, according to me. Do you think I'm lying?" I ask.

Wolf shifts and sits taller. "We all know you are trying to do what's best. That is not the question."

Wind nods and speaks up. "We hear Bird speak…we hear Lib speak. But we must find what is right for the good of the clan."

A shrill laugh bursts out of me. "That's what you're not seeing—there will be no clan if the AI has her way."

Standing, Bird faces the council. "One life can change everything. We know this. We face the loss of Lizard…of Sidewinder. We lose too much. My visions tell me this is the wrong way to go. The gear we bring back with us brings dangers that we cannot win against. Lib says we must battle the AI, but look at the size of the Norm. It fills the horizon. We cannot win against the AI with stolen gear —all we will do is bring more and more drones after us until not one of the Tracker Clan is left alive. I say we need no more biogear."

"So we do nothing? We throw away the biogear that Lizard and Sidewinder died over? We make their deaths mean nothing? The AI has hunted the Rogues for as long as any of you can remember—how can you think the AI will ever allow you to just exist? And what about Tiger and myself—we wore biogear and did not die."

For a moment, no one answers me. My heart is thudding and my stomach churns. My hands shake with the need to make them understand. I'm not seeing agreement from anyone. Lion and Komodo sit with their arms crossed. Wind and Elk won't look up to meet my stare. Wolf's dark eyes seem sad.

A knot tightens in my stomach—have they all made up their minds before this? Is there nothing I can say to make them see the danger of doing nothing?

Bird sits down again and faces me. "We must move beyond this. We must learn that every life is precious—and that sometimes sacrificing even one life means that we have already sacrificed ourselves."

"I don't understand what you're talking about. You're talking as if just going along as you always have is good enough—well, it's not. Do you think this world was always like this? That the Empties were just dumped onto the land already empty and twisted? No…someone made them like that. Someone who didn't want to make sacrifices or see that there was a danger or look ahead to what the future could bring."

"How do you know this?" Komodo says. His words seem grating, as if he's been waiting to say them.

Swallowing hard, I don't know what to answer. Should I tell them of my dreams that I've had—the ones where everyone is dead, killed by the AI? They already know I've connected to the AI before this—that I have a special tie to Conie. If I tell them about the dangers I see will they think I'm just trying to lash out at the AI because of my own fears? My eyes water and a burning spreads over my skin.

Wind looks up and says, "This council is not here to punish Lib. There is much for all of us to think about. Until a decision can be made, I ask the council to agree on no more attacks on drones. Lib can use the biogear she has. But let us see if the gear is calling the drones to us. If it is proven the gear is a danger, we will meet again to decide what must be done."

"And if you tell me I must give up my biogear?" I ask. I'm aware of how it hugs me now, resting against my back, the wires that connect under my skin a little tight right now and the screen turned off at the moment. It feels an extension of me, and I wonder if I'm starting to get more comfortable with it on than I am without it.

Standing, Wind faces me. "If you will not follow law, then you must leave clan."

She walks out. Elk and Bird follow her. Komodo and Lion walk out as well. Horse brushes past me as if I no longer exist, leaving me to face Wolf. I stare at him, hoping he will say something—that the council is wrong, that he believes me when I say we must fight the AI.

He stares at me for a moment, and says, "Change does not come overnight. Use the time you have been given wisely."

Chapter Seven

Hurt and exhausted, I make my way to the women's sleeping quarters. I have skins on the floor in a corner of the room. Right now I just want to go there, curl up and forget this entire day. Use my time wisely—what does that even mean? Am I just supposed to somehow make the biogear wonderful? Or give it up and be more like a Rogue? Should I just pretend I don't know what I know about Conie—how she will go through with her plan to leave this world? So I can just enjoy my last days and go down smiling with everyone else and without a fight?

"That's ridiculous," I mutter aloud and kick at a rock. The council meeting leaves me feeling raw and angry and guilty all at once—which is about how the last one left me.

Would this have happened if I protected Lizard better? Or if Sidewinder had biogear, too?

But what about Bobcat, or even Bear? I was with the clan when they became nonfunctional—when they died. Does that make me responsible for them?

Maybe…or maybe not.

In some ways I feel to blame—but I have always felt as if everything was always my fault. I fear this is something Conie put into me—this need to feel guilty. It is something she can use to try and manipulate me. I know that. But I don't know how to undo it any more than I know how to stop her.

I almost just want to run for the Outside and get as far from the clan as I can—but that is just me being stupid for a moment. I have no wish to die.

The darkness of the tunnels seems almost comforting. My vision has adjusted, and that is not the biogear helping me, it is just that I am used to the darkness. Will I ever get used to others dying? Or am I already too accustomed to that? Is that why I can't cry or even speak for Lizard to remember her?

Am I just callous?

Thinking about it, I know I care about some others. Raj is still an ache in my heart, still a driving need to find him. And Skye—she matters to me, although I do not think I matter very much to her.

And then there is Wolf—even thinking about him, about how he looked at me in the council room, with his eyes dark and cold, leaves my face burning and my stomach churning. He matters—and I cannot undo that.

But as I think of them, each one marks both my mistakes and my successes.

Skye, the first friend I ever made, seems to trust Bird more than me. Wolf took me into the clan, but if it comes to a choice of clan or me, I know he must choose the clan he leads. Raj is—gone. I can only hope he's alive, but it is my fault that Raj never got out of the Norm. I couldn't save him.

If I no longer have the three people who matter the most, I must be doing something wrong. So perhaps Bird has a point about that. But what else should I be doing? How can we win against the AI unless we are ready to die fighting her?

Troubled by my thoughts, I head into the wide chamber set aside for sleep. Most have bedded down for the night and sleep sprawled on their rugs. Glancing around, it takes only a moment to spot Bird and Skye. They sit as far away from where my sleeping skins lay as possible. Bird and Skye once slept beside me. That's changed. A lot has.

Bird glances up as I step into the room. Moonlight barely filters into the room. Bird and Skye are more just dark shapes, with only the flutters of Bird's ribbons and a flash off Skye's pale hair showing where they are. They're too far away for me to hear what they're saying, but their words are a low murmur against the silence of the room.

A pain lodges under my chest, hard and aching. Suddenly, it is too much. I don't want to think about them, I don't want to see them. I don't want to be here. Turning around, I leave, making a point to not look back.

Making a mental list of what I need for a day or so—food, water, extra gear for repairs—I head to the main room. I take one skin of water, a handful of dried meat and cactus fruit will feed me for a day and I can hunt up more after that. Heading to the Gear Room, I light one of the oil lamps with metal and flint that sparks, and hunt up the spare parts I might need.

A small hand on my shoulder stops me and I spin around. I'm surprised to see Skye's golden hair, glinting in the lamp light.

I shake her off her and turn away. "Go back to Bird. Go back to sleep, Skye. Right now, I don't want to see anyone. I've had enough of…of councils."

"Lib, don't be like that." Skye folds her arms over her chest. "I'm not against you. Bird just thinks that—"

"Bird?" I turn and face her. She takes a step back. "When did it become all about you and Bird?"

Skye hesitates and shrugs. "After Raj. We just found we had something in common. We both miss him."

Her words sting. "And I don't?"

"That's not what I meant." She shakes her head. "I only meant that…you've been distant. I know…lots to do with the biogear. And you and Alis seemed to always be here… or you were hanging around Wolf, and he doesn't really like me. But Bird liked Raj and…and he was my first real friend."

"Just like you were mine, but things change." I turn away. "But don't worry. You have Bird. She'll keep you safe in the tunnels. But I've got to go."

She frowns and calls out, "Where?"

Heading out of the Gear Room, I call back, "Don't worry about it. It's nowhere you have to follow."

*   *   *

Heading up to the Outside, I'm grateful the sun is down so the heat isn't blistering like it is in the day. I haven't brought a lot of water with me—it's such a precious resource and I have the clan habits now. Nothing should be wasted, so if anything happens to me, the less water with me, the better. When I need more, I'll connect to get what I need.

Not that I want to deal with the AI right now.

Walking over the dry ground, my boots make no sound. I think over what happened to me when I was able to access the AI mainframe.

The connects we can get from the Outside—from the stations and platforms—are only to secondary systems. But

Raj and I found a way into the Norm, and we got to the Norm's hub. From there, we accessed the AI's mainframe.

We reached straight to Conie.

I don't like thinking about what I found. That information … it all seemed so clinical. Everything I found out about myself made it seem as if I was a test of some kind. Now, I'm beginning to wonder if what she did to me was more extensive than I originally thought.

I'm a Glitch—that is clear. Every Glitch is a Tech that malfunctioned. Somehow, Conie modified me so she could put me in the Outside and use me. I once thought she only used me to locate the Rogues and Glitches she wanted to destroy. Now I'm not so sure. There is more—there must be. Conie manipulated me physically or mentally, and this is why the biogear works better for me than anyone else.

But am I part machine? And was I always this way, or did Conie somehow change me?

My questions leave me not wanting to hack into the AI anytime soon. I also worry about Conie pulling me into a deeper connect like she did—I have no idea how she located me so fast. But if I can't get information from a connect, or the AI, I have somewhere else I can try.

The Empties.

It's good to be out of the tunnels. The sky seems vast, spread with stars that glitter now the moon has set. For some reason, going to the Empties is a comfort to me. The first time I went as a Glitch about to become part of the clan—now I'm going just as Lib looking for answers.

It takes some time to hike to where we hide the ATs—the wheeled vehicles that have a cage on them and a driver's seat. I have to take one to get close to the Empties. The AT can charge during the day and I can return tomorrow night. I flip down the biogear screen so I can scan for drones. So far the night seems quiet.

Pulling off one of the brown cloths that hides the ATs, I climb on and start the motor. It whines to life, the power source boxes humming. Turning it, I head out of the mountains and for the flats.

The sun is just coming up when I spot the bent and twisted towers that jut into the sky. They look almost like bones, like a hand sticking up from the sand. They are outlined by the pale dawn and are just as impressive as I remember. The vast size of the Empties, the twisted shapes, speak to me of loneliness.

I find a small group of stunted trees and bushes outside the Empties and leave the AT there. The Tracker Clan has a habit of never taking an AT into the rows of buildings—I don't know why, but I follow the law on this.

Walking, sweat blooms on my face and sticks my skin tunic to my back. The day is already warming.

As I get closer, the towers change from just dark shapes into the ragged remains of a long-gone civilization. I step into wide, flat land that is covered with something that isn't just dirt. Rogues have scavenged from the Empties for a long time, and now there is only weathered pieces of broken glass or small scraps of metal in sight. You have to go deeper into the ruins to find anything of use.

I wander without a plan. It is good to have some time to myself, but I keep yawning and my steps are dragging.

I slip into a building that still stands and even has a roof and walls. The space is empty and stairs still lead up to a shady corner where I can sleep. Curling up, I fall asleep at once.

The sun wakes me—hot and bright. I'm sweating and must stink a little. But I stand and stretch. Now I'm rested and need to get moving. Something is driving me. I'm here for a reason—something in the depth of my memory stirs, but I'm not sure what.

I'll know when I find it.

Heading back down the stairs, I break into a jog. My biogear lets me run deeper into the Empties than I have ever been before. It's effortless to run, and I glance around me as I go. The tall buildings give way to shorter ones. I glance into some and see broken bits of wood that had been shaped to be functional at one time.

A few vehicles block my path—I can tell they had wheels at one time, but now most of the metal has been pulled off to fashion knives or something else more useful. They seem sad in a way—left behind to be mangled and used only for the metal they once held.

A breeze sweeps past me, warm and stinging sand against my face. Slowing to a walk, I drink some water and then turn down between buildings in an area of the Empties where I have never been before—but, oddly, I feel as if I have been here.

The Empties—or this part of them—suddenly looks a lot like inside the Norm. Instead of green trees, however, dead ones lie across the ground. Instead of grass like in the Norm, the Empties offers up only sand and dust. But the buildings are similar—one and two floors, and some have flat tops and others have peaked tops on them. Heading to a building that looks a lot like the hub of the Norm—the place where I lost Raj—I step inside. A long hall takes me down to a room. Something slaps me in the face and I grab it.

It is like the skin from an animal, but is much thinner and feels smooth and slick as if something coats it—the coating is probably what has kept this from disappearing in sand storms. Faded writing of some kind swirl across the square. I slip it into my pouch.

Nothing is wasted—not even something that might not be of use.

Heading back out of the building, I glance around. I can see nothing of any use—not any gear, or metal I could use or take with me. I keep looking anyway—I have never been here before so why not look?

I step inside other buildings—the ones that don't look ready to fall over or that have not already crumbled into a heap of stone—and I climb several flights of rickety steps in one. I find a metal box. Using Raj's knife, I pry open the lid. I find images of people. They aren't on a screen, but appear on flat material that is like that coated skin I just found.

I pick through them and find crystals attached to metal —some look as if they are rubies or diamonds. Those are always useful in making biogear. Picking up the bits and pieces, I put everything into my pouch. Standing, I make my way carefully back down the stairs. Wood creaks beneath my boots.

Staring at these places, I wonder about the people who must have lived here—I have their images now, or some of them, in my pouch. Were they clan? Did they plan to leave, or did whatever happen occur suddenly?

I wonder if they were like the Tracker Clan council—did they not want to see the trouble coming at them. Were they happy just to keep living, and did they not want to face hard choices and sacrifices? Or did they adopt every new thing? Is Bird right to worry? I just don't know about that. But how else can we fight if not with the biogear?

Nothing else inside any building seems of use. I end up back where I started, aware that the sun is now stretching long shadows from the buildings.

Turning, I retrace my steps. The shifting light reflects golden off something—metal. Turning, I head into what seems to be some sort of storage space. It looks as if other clans have been here and gathered things of use, but never came back for them. I find two rolls of copper wire, which I grab, one screen that isn't cracked and a power supply box. They leave my pouch heavy on my shoulder.

Stepping back into the sun, I see it is dipping. Nights get cold and I have no skins to wrap around me, and I dare not light a fire. Drones might see it. I scan the sky. So far no drones. Either they don't really care or track the biogear, or they don't ever come near the Empties. I'm not sure which is true.

And I haven't found what I'm looking for...yet.

*   *   *

It's nightfall by the time I climb down into the tunnels. I leave the AT hidden under its cloth, and stop five times on the way back to make certain no drones are following. The tunnels seem empty, so the clan must be at the evening meal—almost everyone gathers for that. I ate the food I took with me hours ago, but I am not willing to face everyone to eat. I drink my water and head to the Gear Room.

I have no idea if anything I collected is of use. Maybe the wire—it can at least be made into a bracelet or can wrap the hilt of a knife. If this was an official scavenge, I'd call it a waste of time. But now I wonder if that is a good phrase.

Can time be wasted?

I'm feeling calmer—less angry. So even if I did not find much in gear, I found some perspective. And my biogear did not attract any drones to me.

I'm just pulling off my pouch and pulling out the screen I brought back when Bird steps into the Gear Room.

The calm I found threatens to leave me, but I manage to ask, "What do you want?"

She pushes the ribbons in her hair back from her face. "What do you think you'll find out there?" Her glance shifts to my pouch. "In the Empties. That's where you went. That gear could only have come from there, and Skye said you left when you weren't supposed to. What do you think you'll find?"

I clear my throat and straighten. "Why are you asking? What—do you want to drag me in front of the council and tell them I went out with my biogear on?"

She frowns. "Do you want to die? Is that why you do things like this?"

I turn away, but she says, "Don't worry, I won't tell anyone. What does it matter if you go there by yourself? At least you're only putting yourself in danger."

"That's right. It's just me. But...I didn't see a single drone out there. They aren't coming after the biogear."

Her eyes narrow. She turns and walks away.

Turning to the wood I have set up, I dump out the things I scavenged. I pry the crystals out of the metal. I can use the metal—if I can get a hot enough fire going, I can melt the metal and use it again. And the crystals will help me make another set of biogear. But it is the images of the people that draw my attention. The images are so faded I can barely make out the clothes and faces. I'm still not certain why I even brought them back.

The images appear to be part of the odd skin that they are on. I try burning an edge and it burns like wood. So it must be made from wood or something like that. Some images show one person, some show two or more, and I think these must be clan. Others images seem to be cut out of larger ones.

Pulling out the other slick material—the one with letters —I stare at it. As a Tech, I must have known how to read, but these words seem unfamiliar…and yet…

I flip down the biogear screen and activate it with a thought. For an instant, the biogear seems to be scanning, and then the biogear slips the words into my mind as if someone was speaking them.

The closure of the Board of Emissions is expected to create a rise in greenhouse gases. Warming trends cannot be reversed. The Normandy Project promises salvation in the form of domes that will be constructed over major cities to maintain computer controlled climates.

Dr. Constance Sig head of the project said, "There is no guarantee—and we may have to opt to combined domes for greater efficiency due to the speed at which climates are changing. But the Control Over the Normal Inhabited Environment is a huge...

Conie—Control Over the Normal Inhabited Environment. The AI told me that was her name, but that she liked Conie better. My face goes numb and for a moment I can't seem to breathe.

Conie—she was created to control the Norm. To make it safe. And someone named Dr. Sig had created her—so Dr. Sig must have made a way to shut her down.

Staring at the words, I wished I had more. What were these greenhouse gases? And why did the climate change?

Were there once many domes? Why was there only the Norm now?

"Lib, there you are."

Alis's voice makes me jump. I turn and put a hand over the images of the people. I'm afraid she'll see it and she, too, will know I went to the Empties on my own, even though the council said no one should leave the tunnels.

She doesn't even notice the images, but goes straight for the copper wire and screen. "These don't look like drone parts."

"No. They're...different."

She looks at me sideways. Her red hair hangs loose and curling around her face. "Did you get them in the Empties? Skye keeps saying I should go, but I don't see why."

"You need to go. It's how you're officially initiated into the Tracker Clan."

"I know. I know." She wrinkles her nose. "But I can be clan without really being clan. I'm happy just to be a Glitch, really. Although, sometimes I really miss the Norm."

"The Empties—it's a lot like the Norm. But…drier. Browner."

She gives me a look from the corner of her eyes. "And a long trek just to see empty buildings. I know almost all the good gear has been scavenged. Skye said so."

"Yeah, well, Skye says a lot of things. You should go and see for yourself."

Leaning her shoulder against the stone wall, she asks me, "So why are you really going there? Is it a great place to meet up with a guy?" She grins.

I don't smile back at her. I start to organize the wire I brought back. "A place that's deserted is an easy place to think. You don't have to meet anyone."

"Ah, still having issues with Wolf?"

Glancing at her, I tell her, "More like issues with the council. I just…I don't like the direction they're thinking about going."

She nods. "The biogear. I've heard talk about how we don't really need gear. Maybe…now I don't know if anyone's thought this, but if we do give up our biogear, there could be more drones than ever."

Turning, I raise my eyebrows and stare at her. "What do you mean?

"Well, think about it. By now the AI has figured out we're killing its drones. Rogues typically just hide, so we are atypical. The AI must track how many drones it makes and how many are destroyed. If the destruction rate goes up, why not increase production to compensate?"

I think about this for a long moment. "There is always the factor of resources. Drone manufacturing requires raw materials. It's quite possible the AI doesn't have sufficient resources. Or power."

Alis nods. "That may be a factor. But the AI has the Norm."

I start to smile. "And if we take out drones—this could be another way to slow down the AI's plans. I mean, if the AI is focused on making drones to replace the ones we take out, she can't be using those resources to get ready to leave for space. We have a possible delaying tactic." I thump a fist onto the wood. "But only if we keep going after the AI."

Alis lets out a long breath. "Yeah, that's the trick isn't it? We go after the drones, what happens first—do we all die, one at a time? Or do we pull enough resources away. Doesn't seem the best plan since we don't really know."

She's right about that.

My stomach makes a gurgling noise. I can't ignore my hunger any longer. Telling Alis I'm going to get something to eat, I head out.

I put the images of the people and the text the biogear helped me read into my pouch. I leave my biogear behind, a little itchy once it disconnects, and I leave Alis tinkering with a new biogear pack.

Only a few of the clan—just three—linger off water and food. I find a bowl of dried fruit and take it to a spot near a wall where I usually sit.

Wolf comes in with Tiger, both of them talking quietly and intently. I focus on my fruit, and draw in the packed dirt at my feet with a finger. After I eat, I pull out the images again and look through them.

The last one stops me. It is faded, but shows a woman with dark hair pulled back and a small smile. I know those high cheekbones and that narrow chin. Pain spikes my chest.

This is the woman's face that Conie projects when she takes on a physical form. This is the face that could be my mother's face. Below the image is tiny writing. I no longer have the biogear to help me read it, but these letters are the same as ones that the biogear read to me.

This is the face of Dr. Constant Sig.

Chapter Eight

Dr. Constance Sig.

Constance...Conie?

Is the AI naming herself after her creator?

The image is a tangible connection between Dr. Sig and the artificial intelligence that controls the Norm. But the information that the biogear helped me read indicated there were other domes—not just one. Were they all put together? Dr. Sig said that might need to be done. But why is there just one Norm? Did the AI decide that had to be done? Were the other domes all smashed? Maybe there was once a dome over the Empties—but it is gone now.

I don't know what Normandy means, but I know that *Norm* is. Is it possible that the scientists working on the project succeeded, but not the way they had intended?

All of this seems to leave me with more questions. However, I have two new facts I can use—the biogear can help me understand old information that has been left behind. This may lead to a discovery for how to fight the

AI. And…I now know a little more about the AI. It was created, and that means there is a way to destroy it as well.

This is more exciting than anything else. My heart is beating faster and my breaths come quickly. This is real information about where the AI came from.

Taking a deeper breath, I know I'm going to have to be careful of how I go about explaining what I know. Already the others doubt me. It is possible this will just be more of me trying to tell the others what I know and having them doubt me because no one else has read this—or even seen the AI's face.

And I will have to explain how I came by this knowledge.

I told Wolf about what happened to me inside the Norm, about my confrontation with the AI, and how Raj disappeared. But I didn't tell him everything. How could I explain how she seemed so familiar to me…and how part of me wanted to stay with her.

I have no family that I remember, but the few memories I have include this woman's face as she smiles at me and talks to me. This could be only a memory of the AI—she turned me into a Glitch, after all. And the AI sent me to the Outside to find the other Glitches. But I have a hope now that maybe I am really remembering a descendant of Dr. Sig—and that woman is my real mother. It is possible that a daughter, or a daughter's daughter, could look like Dr. Sig. I want to believe I have a connection with a real person, and not just with the AI.

I haven't told anyone any of this, but if anyone can understand me it is Wolf.

Hope sparks inside me, and it brings the desire to find this other woman who looks like Dr. Sig. I have to talk to someone, and I must talk to Wolf about my discoveries.

Getting up, I head to try and find Wolf.

It takes some time, but eventually I follow the tunnels and pointers from two others who say Wolf is training.

We use two training areas—one in the Outside where we can train with the ground above, and then tunnels that are wide enough to allow training underground. The training space is kept bare, with sand and dirt for the floor—it makes falling a little softer. Training is always two of the clan practicing fight moves—but I really need to make a dummy drone that we could train against. That is our real enemy.

The training room is wide enough to easily hold about half the clan—a dozen of us could train in here. However, I see Wolf and Bird at once, circling each other. Two others of the clan hang back, watching. Light spills down from the hole in the center of the room. Wolf moves in and out of the light. His arms are bare—his tunic only covers his chest—his skin pants tight, and his boots make no sound on the soft dirt.

He moves fast. He does not need biogear to be dangerous. He trained me to be strong, and I will never forget that.

I watch him a moment longer, appreciating the tautness of his muscles and the ease in every move. For someone so big, he moves like one of his namesakes. Like a big wolf. Slipping into the training area, I hug the wall, watching.

Bird lets out a lighthearted laugh. I haven't heard such a laugh in a long time. The ribbons tied through her thick hair flutter as she hops from foot to foot. She says something that I can't catch and he smiles.

In the next instant, she spins and tries a kick. Wolf dodges, turns and slaps out with one hand. Bird ducks beneath him. He rounds on her, but he is still smiling. They are both sweating and breathing hard. I can see Wolf is enjoying this—so is Bird.

Biting my lower lip, I think about how I haven't trained with Wolf in far too long. That is more my fault than his.

One of the clan sitting on the ground and watching calls out to Wolf to step it up. Bird swats at Wolf and tries to hit him with another wheeling kick.

Wolf dodges and gets a slap in on her leg.

Turning away, I leave. I don't want to watch them anymore. And I can't talk to Wolf with Bird around—she'll make me doubt myself. She'll make Wolf doubt me.

I have to talk to someone, but I have no idea who now.

Skye…well, Skye will listen, but she'll tell Bird and that won't help. Alis will listen, too, but she won't be able to help me with plans for what to do next—Alis just thinks everything I do is great, and that's not really any help.

Raj would have helped me.

A sharp pang tightens around my chest. There are times I turn a corner in the tunnels, or head to the main room, and almost expect Raj to be there, with his dark, curling hair, deep eyes, that crooked smile of his that said he knew things no one else did. I don't miss his moody attitude, but I do miss his determination.

He was sure we could fix the AI, and then we could all live in the Norm where it is green and there is always enough water.

Raj believed I am somehow special. Raj listened to me.

My eyes sting and wet trickles down my cheek. I brush it away.

I should have gone back for him. I should go back for him.

Staggering to a halt, I slap one hand against the wall to steady myself.

I should go back for him.

Instantly a dozen problems hit me.

I don't know if Raj is alive—or if he is still in the Norm. I am not certain I can hack a way back into the Norm—

when I did that before, the AI still wanted me to be alive. That has changed.

But I can't shake the idea that Raj must be alive still. I never saw his body—I only saw that he was no longer helping me try to fix the AI. We failed at that. I don't want to fail Raj again.

So I need a better plan.

*   *   *

I have no doubt that Wolf will never approve any plan to get inside the Norm again—I almost died. And right now the council doesn't want anyone heading to the Outside with biogear. I am going to need my biogear to save Raj. And I still need to tell Wolf—somehow—about what I've learned about the AI and being able to read old information from the biogear.

That leaves my thoughts and emotions tangling. Wolf never liked Raj—in fact, a lot of the clan didn't like him. But Raj might know more about the AI now—that alone is a good reason to try and get him back.

I have to remember, though, how hard it was to escape the Norm last time. I almost didn't make it out. Inside the Norm, the AI controls everything—the human Techs, the drones, and the sentinels that project the mainframe as well. Wolf won't want me trying something he will see as certain death. I am not looking forward to this either.

But there's more to consider.

I have no idea where to begin.

The Norm is not as big as the Outside, but it still has a lot of tall buildings and a lot of places to hide. This will be good if Raj is hiding from the AI—it is not so good for me when it comes to looking for Raj.

If I can locate him, I might stand a chance. We might stand a chance.

But I'm going to need some way to hide us from the AI. Maybe I can use the biogear to make the other drones think I am a drone, too. Which means I'll need a pack of biogear for Raj, too.

Heading to the Gear Room, I see Alis is working on her biogear. Dat is slumped over with his back to the wall and is snoring softly. A skin rug covers him—probably Alis looking after him.

Heading over to Alis, I glance at the biogear she has spread out.

Alis glances up and blows out a long breath. She is clearly not happy. "I just can't get my biogear to get its screen to activate. I've looked over all of your wiring and duplicated it. I just don't understand. What am I doing wrong?"

"There is always an answer. It may not have anything to do with you doing something wrong. I think it's a biological thing...this isn't just gear. We're making gear connection with each of us."

Raj always thought I was different.

Picking up some of the copper wiring I brought back from the Empties, I pull over one of the oil lamps. "You're different from me...so let's try some different wiring."

Alis starts to strip out the wires she has for the main connection in her biogear. "So, have you worked things out with Wolf?"

I glance at her. "He's training with Bird. Hard to talk to him when he's with her."

"Or is it just hard to talk to him?" Alis asks.

I wave for her to pull her biogear closer. We start to change out the wires, replacing the drone wiring with the copper from the Empties. "Hard and getting harder it seems like. It's been...different since that council meeting. Maybe I was wrong about him."

Alis stabs her thumb on a wire. She sticks it into her mouth, sucks on it and then pulls it out and asks, "Or maybe he was wrong—or the council was. Isn't there some old saying about that's how you know who is human—they make mistakes?"

I flash her a smile and shrug. "So if I'm right I'm not human. That's not comforting."

Alis grins now. We finish rewiring her biogear, and she runs a hand over the black shell that will attach to her back. "I can't wait to try this out. And...and of course you're human. What else would you be?"

I shrug, but the word different keeps echoing in my head.

Turning from the biogear, I tell Alis, "Maybe Wolf and I...maybe he isn't right for me...or maybe it's that I'm not right." Waving at her biogear, I tell her. "Go ahead and put it on. We need to train more with our biogear, so let's do some of that."

Alis's eyes widen. "Right here? Now?"

"Why not? We've got room enough here to try some moves and tests."

She nods, picks up her biogear and slings it onto her back. Fastening the straps, she says, "You know, if it means anything, I think Wolf is stuck in the old ways."

I frown. I don't agree with her, but I'm starting to think Wolf is caught between the old ways of the council and what we're going to have to do—how we're going to have to change—to fight the AI. Wolf told me that change doesn't happen fast—so he knows change needs to happen. But he must hate seeing those he's known for all his life die —I would hate that.

Alis slips on her biogear. It gives a soft hum and activates. She grins. I give her a nod and have her start to test the functions—strength, speed, screen. Everything seems to work. And a certainty settles into me.

Maybe because I have so few connection to the clan that allows me to function in ways they can't. I can take leaps ahead, where they are stuck with how they've always done things, and with the fear of losing close friends. I have so very little to lose. Watching Alis test her biogear solidifies my decision to go after Raj. He is a connection I have and I have waited too long to go after him.

If he's alive, I'll save him. Even if that means I must give up the clan—and even if that means Wolf and I have to part ways, too.

Chapter Nine

I wake early with the intent of scavenging in the Empties. I need to find more information on the AI. I might also find out more about Dr. Sig—and I want to test more of the biogear. I've made adjustments to enhance the screen and I need more gear to see if I can modify this to better hide me from the AI. That is going to be vital to find and save Raj.

The real problem, however, is how to access the Norm again.

Having something to do makes me feel lighter—there is less time to think about Wolf or Bird or everything else. I want to focus on my task.

I pack lightly—a few pieces of dried meat and a skin of water. My biogear slips on like a warm coat on a cold night —it seems heavy in my hand, but when I shrug it onto my back, it seems to weigh nothing then. Slinging a pouch over my shoulder, I head for one of the exits. Just ahead, dim light from early dawn drifts down into the tunnels. I make a quick check of my biogear, but when I look up I see Wolf standing in front of me, blocking the way to the exit.

He towers over me, though I'm not short. As I look up at his wide shoulders and his dark eyes, I wonder if I should tell him about my discoveries, but the words dry up. Will he believe me? Will he think I am making connections that aren't there?

I don't know if Wolf really can understand what it is I need to do—but I do know that if Wolf tries to stop me, he can't. The biogear makes me as strong as he is—maybe even stronger.

"What do you think you're doing?" His voice is soft, but I can hear irritation, and something else. He sounds a little worried.

I take a deep breath. *None of your business,* sounds like a really good response in my head, but I know it's not. Wetting my lips, I take another breath and tell him, "Out. I have things to do."

"This is how you use the time the council gave you?"

"The council gave me nothing—they want to take everything away. But this is my choice. I'm going out. By myself. I've done it before, and no drones showed up. So I'm not putting the clan in danger." Lifting my chin, I fix a stare on him, challenging him to try and stop me.

His dark eyes narrow. His face seems to tighten. "What's out there? What's the point? And you are clan—so you going out there means you aren't safe."

I shake my head. "I'm not really sure I am clan—not anymore. Maybe I never was."

Arms dropping to his sides and his voice dropping low, he asks, "How can you say that? You eat with us—sleep with us."

"This is just the place that took me in when I didn't know who I was—or even what I was. And…and there are people here I care for—" I look up at him and keep my stare on him. "But some don't want me here. And don't trust me. So I have to do this on my own."

"Bird is just—"

"This isn't about Bird. I understand that she blames me, but she is just one. Think about the council—they looked at me with suspicion, they think the biogear is bad. But I'm not going to put away the only tools we have to fight back."

"What—is this about Rogues and Glitches again? You're a Glitch, and so you can never be a Rogue? Is that why you say you aren't clan?"

Throwing my hands wide, I tell him, "No…it's about the gear. Rogues have worn it—Lizard put it on. Glitches take to the biogear faster, but it doesn't matter who wears the gear. What matters is that the council is ready to throw it away because of a fear—because it's different."

"Because it makes us not quite human?" Wolf rubs a hand over his face. When he looks at me again, he just looks young and a little lost. "I told you change does not come overnight—I meant that. You have to give the clan time to get used to new ideas—to this gear."

"I wish I could. I wish we had lots and lots of time. But we don't know how much time there is. The AI is doing things and we aren't keeping track of her close enough. We hang back and we hide and we try to live under the shadow of the Norm. Those shadows vanish if the AI takes the Norm into space—and she will. Even if the council doesn't believe me—even if you don't believe me—that won't stop it from happening."

"What if I ask you to stay?" Wolf says, his voice so soft I almost don't hear the words.

For a long time I stare up at him, letting my gaze slide along the lines of his face. Three tiny scars, from fights with animals and drones, run together on his right cheek, near the corner of his mouth. Lines from worry and frowning cross his forehead. He's handsome—I've always thought that—but I forget sometimes he must rule the clan, but he is almost as young as I am. A weight seems to pull at his shoulders. Sometimes I wonder if he was ready for his role, or if bears it because, like me, he has no other choice.

His solid endurance makes me like him more, but I have to remember he doesn't know everything. It seems so easy —so tempting to just lean on him. To listen to his council. I want to ask him for help—but now I see how unfair that would be to him. He has his own problems and is trying to do his best with them.

I have to do the same.

Standing straighter, I tell him, "If you don't want me to come back, I won't come back. I'm not backing down from a fight with the AI."

His shoulders jerk almost like I've hit him. He looks shocked by my words, and I have to admit they taste bitter. I've only wanted to belong here—but now I see Raj was right in a way I never understood before now.

My being different might be the one thing that saves us all.

"I have to go," I mutter. Pushing past him, I head down the tunnel and for the exit overhead. A rope will allow me to pull myself up to the Outside.

Wolf calls out, "At least tell me where are you headed?"

I glance back. In the dim light that leaks down, I can't see his expression. My heart gives a hard thump—at least he asked. Turning away, I tell him, "The Empties."

"Why?" he asks.

I say the first thing that comes to mind. "To find answers."

Wolf doesn't say anything and doesn't follow.

I climb up with the rope we use to exit the tunnels. Outside the wind is chilly. The sun has not yet fully risen, but a band of pale gray sky shows it will soon. I settle my empty pouch and turn to the far mountains.

Nothing lives in the Empties, but that doesn't mean there is nothing there. The clans scavenge the Empties for metal, for parts, but now I head there for something else that can be gained—information.

If I can learn about Dr. Sig and the AI, maybe I can learn about my own family, too.

The idea seems almost ridiculous even in my own head, but the hope beats in me as steady as my footsteps.

I told Wolf the truth—I will find my answers.

*   *   *

Leaving the ATs means walking, but it is a chance to test the biogear's power and endurance. I settle into a steady jog.

As soon as the sun comes up, the Outside becomes hot. As always. There are seasons, as the clan calls them. A season of rain, which means clouds and heat and water that dries almost before it hits the ground. A season of cold winds from the north that blow every day. A season of extra heat when the sun seems to beat down with almost an intent to kill, and the clan goes out then only at night. And this season—the season of change, when the winds are fitful and sometimes clouds fill the sky, and the dust storms come up sudden and fierce.

Within the Norm, I have a faint memory of every day being the same as the last. This makes sense if a dome protects the Norm and the AI keeps a perfect, climate controlled environment. This is what that writing the biogear helped me read spoke of—a perfect climate in order to survive. Meaning the Outside is not a place where very much can live.

And yet, trees struggle to grow and brush manages to put out leaves, and animals survive. The Outside is stark and seems bare at first glance, but I have learned to listen to the sounds and pay attention to where the snakes like to find warmth and the animals like to hunt.

I have also been inside the Norm and even if it looks beautiful on the surface, I know it is a place where the AI controls the minds of those within it. How can someone without the control over their own mind really be happy? How can they be anything except what the AI wants them to be?

The heat washes over me, slowly baking my skin which has gotten steadily darker since the day I woke up here, parched and alone. My hair has gotten lighter, too, as a result of the exposure to elements outside of the dome. There are golden streaks in it that I can only barely see when I tug at the tips of the shorter strands. Skye has told me she thinks they give me a sunny look. I don't think too much about them.

As I head to the Empties, Wolf's words linger. I can hear what he did not say—the concern in his tone, the worry, the fear. I have some of my own. Wolf and I seem to be parting paths. I don't want this, but I cannot give up my fight with the AI. I will not give up fighting to know more. And I have a task—a need to save Raj.

Ahead, the silhouetted Empties crop up in the distance. They look a long distance away, thanks to the heat waves lifting from the ground and the distortions of sun and shadow.

I put one foot in front of the other, my throat dry, keeping to a steady jog. The ground shimmers and shifts beneath my feet. Colors seem to fracture in the sunlight until the golden browns of the Outside shift and become dark purple, then blue and cool.

And as soon as I notice it, the world shifts. It is just like before, with the biogear connecting me to another place. In the next step, I'm jogging down a corridor, blue tiles beneath my boots.

The Empties disappear as does the Outside. A long hallway tinted in the blue that marks the world of the AI stretches out in front of me. Fibers of light line the edges of the floor and the walls, giving off a soft glow. Stopping, heart thudding against my ribs, I look down at my hands. The soft lighting makes my skin look pale again and smoother than it really is now.

Go back. Wake up. Do something.

But what?

The hall slips past me, even though I am not moving. A door appears at the end of the hall, heading toward me. My heart thumps loudly, filling my ears with a steady thud.

I reach for the door, my hand steady despite how my insides shake. I slide my palm over the smooth, polished surface of the knob.

Curiosity and the need to know pulse through me and I know I will open the door. I know everything will change. But how do I—

The vision blinks out as if it never happened. Again, I'm in the Outside, the Empties in front of me, the ruined towers and the skeleton-like structures black and twisted.

A shiver runs through me.

I don't know what's wrong with me—or what's wrong with the biogear. Is the AI able to connect to it in a way I don't understand? Or is the biogear accessing my memories?

All I do know is that hallway belongs to the AI…and I worry that somehow she is still controlling me.

Chapter Ten

The Empties yield a few more of the coated sinks and I learn they are called papers and have been sealed with something once called plastic. I find those words on one of the squares. There is a great deal of information, but much of it seems concerned with details of life that make no sense to me out of the context for when they were created. I find nothing more about Dr. Sig or Conie. Nothing on what happened to the Empties or how the Norm became the only dome that survived the terrible events that left the Outside so dry and barren.

Returning to the tunnels, I half expect to be told I cannot come back to the clan. But Wolf has left Gazelle at the tunnel entrance, waiting for me, and Gazelle gives me a nod and water—my own skin is empty. Young and fresh-faced, Gazelle doesn't ask me where I've been or if I have been out on a scavenge. She is kind enough to me that I give her two of the pretty stones I found in the Empties. I don't say anything about the squares with information that I found. I'm tired enough that I sleep away most of the day.

At evening meal, Wolf gives me a long, hard stare as if he wants to know what I have been doing and why I keep going back to the Empties. It's hard to ignore his unhappy frowns, but I do my best. Maybe I should just be happy that he's even looking at me after the words we exchanged.

For the next few days, I spend my time in the Gear Room. Dat has working biogear at last, and has some ideas to try and set up communications between the biogear packs. I worry that the AI or other drones could tap into those communications. But Dat's idea leads me to another one that might be something we can use to confuse them. If we broadcast empty sounds—noise that is meaningless, a jarring hiss—that might leave the drones unable to talk to the AI or to each other. If their communications are taken up with this noise, that might help get me into the Norm since the AI won't be able to order them to stop me. It is an idea worth working on and one I can dive into.

On the third morning at the early meal in the main room, Alis comes up to me with an offer of meat roasted on a stick. It smells good and my stomach grumbles. I take a bite, and Alis sits down next to me. "I heard council has told Wolf to set up a scavenge for tonight."

Staring at her, the meat going cold on its stick, I ask, "Did they say if biogear can be worn? Who they'll be sending?"

She shrugs and shakes her head. "Don't know. Just heard Skye talking about it when she washed in the hot springs." She snorts. "My guess is no biogear."

I'm surprised she thinks that. Alis, Dat and myself have been the only ones working on biogear. Dat and I have been immersed in trying to make the biogear put out a steady noise on all the commutations channels we can find, but so far we haven't made much progress. It's left me frustrated that I can't make the idea work, can't find how the drones talk to each other, but I'm unwilling to give up on it. Even though I've heard talk that the biogear is a waste of time—it seems Bird and Wolf aren't the only ones who don't like having gear here.

Ever since Lizard died, most of the clan doesn't even want to look at the biogear. Only Crow has come by once or twice to see what we're doing.

It didn't kill Lizard—and Sidewinder died too, without any gear.

Heading to the Gear Room, I slip on my biogear and head to the space set aside for training. I need to work on showing the others the biogear does work—and it doesn't call drones. I've been out now to the Empties several times and not a single drone has come after me.

But I worry a little. Is the AI watching me? Does she know I'm by myself and so she doesn't send drones because she wants to attack a larger group?

My nerves and anticipation for a scavenge tonight all seem to come out in the otherwise empty training room. The biogear lets me move fast—but I push it, trying to punch even faster and harder. I have new metal on my hands that lets me punch into rock, but the vibration rattles up my arm, leaving my joints aching. I need to reinforce the metal. Working up a sweat drains some of my tension. Breathing hard, I lean against the cool stone walls and stare at the dirt floor.

Will Wolf ask me to come on the scavenge—and if he does should I go with my biogear on despite what the council has said?

I'm surprised when Skye strolls into the training area, her steps light and her hair pale in the dim light leaking down from the hole in the ceiling. She offers me a smile, which I hesitantly return. We haven't been spending a lot of time together lately and I feel badly for that, but I'm not to be blamed for the distance growing between us.

"Hey," she says, her voice small and tentative. Clearing her throat, she says, "You heard about the scavenge tonight? Wolf's making plans right now for it."

Straightening, I ask, "Where is he? Did he send for me?"

She frowns and shrugs again. "Everyone's in the main room. Wolf wants everyone there."

I brush the sweat off my forehead. I must smell and dirt streaks my hands. It might be best for me to take off my biogear, but I follow Skye back to the main room.

Skye heads over to sit by Bird, but I hang back in the shadows of the tunnel. The talk is ordinary—Wolf wants two teams to head out for a water scavenge. But instead of going for a connect to get water from the Norm, Wolf wants the teams to scavenge water from the few plants that store it—the prickly ones he calls cactus.

Clenching my jaw, desperation wells in me. I have no place on a scavenge like this—I'd only be of use on a connect. And Wolf tells everyone no biogear—just knives and ATs for the scavenge. It feels like a dagger being plunged into my chest.

Not only am I not needed, the council still thinks the biogear is a problem, not our only hope. And Wolf seems to think that, too.

Turning away, I head to the hot springs. The ones in this tunnel aren't as hot as the ones we had in the old tunnels. I don't use them often—some of the clan will go and soak if Croc tells them they have to for strained muscles. But I tend just to wash fast.

The hot springs are at the far end of the tunnels, and I stop and strip off my biogear and boots. I keep a square of cloth from my old tunic that I had on when I was thrown out of the Norm and I dip that into the steaming water and wash off. Then sit with my feet soaking in the hot water.

How can I convince Wolf and the council the biogear is a necessary tool—that it is safe? My wearing it doesn't seem to make a difference to anyone. If only Wolf would try it out.

Thinking about Wolf—how he doesn't seem to need biogear to be fast and strong—almost seems to call him to the hot springs. He steps into the room, stops and then heads over to where I'm sitting. He pulls off his shirt as he comes inside, dropping it to the floor. His pants go next.

My face heats and I look away. After the soft rustle of skin pants hitting the stone floor, water splashes. Looking up, I see Wolf, his shoulders and chest—bare and glistening. Water covers the rest of him, and steam weaves up around his face, making his long hair curl on the ends.

"Problems?"

I shake my head and stand. "No new ones." Heading over to my boots and biogear, I grab them and then glance at Wolf. "It's a mistake not to use the biogear."

He lifts a shoulder and lets it drop. Water swirls around him, and my mouth dries. I'm tempted to strip off my clothes and step into the warm water with him just to see

141

what he would do. The ache to feel his arms around me holds me still—I don't want to need anyone like that. "We'll see. If the drones come, we'll know it's not the biogear calling them."

"Like anyone will believe that—they'll just find another reason to throw the gear out." Turning, I head into the tunnel before Wolf can say anything else—or before the urge to stay keeps me too close to him.

Working with Dat on hooking up a noise broadcaster keeps me busy. We've found how the drones talk, with short waves of sound. I'm almost too busy to think about Wolf or the scavenge tonight.

But at the evening meal, Skye comes over to me and sits next to me. She hasn't eaten with me in a very long time. She pops a chunk of meat into her mouth—we have snake for dinner tonight—chews, swallows and then says, "You've been quiet lately." Her voice sounds forced, as if she's trying to be cheerful. "I know you've been going out on your own. Everyone knows."

I look at her sideways and think about my answer. Should I tell her what I found in the Empties? How the biogear lets me read the old writing, and how I have proof there were once other domes, other Norms, but they're all gone. How I know that Conie—the AI—took her name from her creator, Dr. Sig? But what good will it do? Skye will nod and listen, but she likes to follow. She can't help anyone lead. She can't help me make the others see that we have to start planning how to fight the AI.

I smile and wave a hand. "I'm not on this scavenge." I try not to look at Wolf who is dressed and sitting next to Bird and Lion, eating as they talk. My skin warms, just as it always does when I stare at him.

Skye seems to follow my gaze because she says, "Because of Bird?"

"Could be. Also probably because of Wolf now. And the biogear I use." My anger sits heavy in my stomach. I hand the rest of my food to Dat, who always seems to be hungry.

For a moment Skye chews her meat and then she speaks up again. "Bird doesn't hate you."

I raise a single eyebrow at her and press my lips together.

"What? It's true," Skye says. "She's just scared. You're changing a lot of things and, well, some of the clan thinks not all of the changes are the right kind."

"Right? There's a right when we're fighting for survival?" I ask.

She looks away. Picking up the stick used to roast the snake meat, she draws little symbols in the sand. I wonder if she remembers how to read—she once was a Tech, before she had problems with her seizures and was declared a Glitch and thrown out of the Norm. She didn't have her memory wiped. The symbols look like lines and circles—data, I realize. She can read data. But what she is drawing is random code—it's meaningless.

"What do *you* think?" I finally ask. My throat tightens. I'm not sure I want to know the answer, but I want her to think for herself.

She hesitates and my stomach drops. "You never stop by the Gear Room to look at the biogear. You think they're not really doing anything for us, don't you?"

She offers me a guilty, lopsided smile. "A lot of what you've done is great. It's just…" She trails off, looking back to the dirt and her drawings.

"Just what? We've destroyed more drones lately than the clan ever did before I came. We've had a lot of successful connects—meaning no one is dying of thirst. We could strike back at the AI—we need to. I thought you knew that."

She winces. "Isn't that the problem, Lib? Going after the AI just makes the AI come after us."

"Oh? Like the AI wasn't trying to wipe out all the Rogues long before I came up with biogear? That's not even close to the truth. And let me remind you that Raj was trying to fix the AI—Raj was willing to fight the AI and die trying if that's what it took."

At the mention of Raj, she bites her lower lip. Her eyes well with moisture. She sucks in a sharp breath and turns her face away. I can see how painful it is for her to think of him.

A knot of guilt tightens in my stomach. Most of the time I'm so wrapped up in how I feel about Raj and what happened to him, that I forget how Skye knew him for a lot longer. Missing him has to be hard on her. Really hard.

Looking up, she manages a bright smile. "All this talk about getting rid of the AI. I'm not sure we'd be alive without the Norm—we get a lot of food and water from the connects."

"Not tonight, we won't," I mutter

Skye shakes her head and tugs on the ends of her pale hair. "Maybe you should just…put away the biogear for a time."

"You mean until Bird approves?"

Back stiff, Skye stares at me, her sky-blue eyes pale. "It's not just her. I've heard others talk about how it isn't natural. Croc worries that it changes your…your biology."

"So what if it does. We're supposed to leave it off and not use everything we can to fight the AI? Gear is just gear —it's a tool, the same way a knife is or fire. And if biogear is bad does that make Techs bad, too, because the AI modified the Techs? And that means Glitches—Techs gone wrong—are bad, too. Don't you see how there is no end to heaping blame? All this means is that only the Rogues—those born outside—are okay and so the Rogues can keep on living like they always have. Except they can't. The AI is going to leave with the Norm and none of us are going to be alive if that happens. But, no, let's stick our heads down in the tunnels and just hope that's not really going to happen because only Lib talked to the AI about the AI's plans."

Bitterness leaks into my voice. I can't hold it back. I'm frustrated Skye can't see the truth—she was a Tech. She should know how heartless the AI can be. Conie is a machine—a thing. Conie doesn't care how many she has to kill to make her plans happen.

Skye surprises me by making a snort as if she thinks I'm making too big a deal about everything. "Gear is different. All that biogear comes from drones that are made by the AI. Maybe wearing it does change us. And you've changed if you can't see that."

"You're right. I have changed. I want to change. We all have to change. We're fighting a war, one that no one seems to want to see. But you...I thought you'd know better. Or is it just that you don't want to lose the Norm? I know you talked to Raj about going back—he told me once you'd talked about that. What…are you afraid that if we destroy the AI, the Norm will be lost, too, and there will never be a chance for you to go back?"

She winces and reaches for my hand. "That is just mean, Lib."

I stand. I've had enough of this conversation. I jerk my hand away from Skye's, I turn away and head to the Gear Room.

It's the only place where I know no one will tell me I'm wrong about everything.

*   *   *

You've changed.

Skye's words linger in my mind. I've added the noise blocker to my biogear and to Alis's but they have not been tested. I still have two more packs to work on and upgrade, and I want to start work on a new, third biogear pack. But I just don't have the energy or enthusiasm for the work.

I wonder if I should go and find Wolf. I still haven't told him what I've found out about the AI, and even if he scoffs or ignores me, he should know. He is the leader—and if anything ever happens to me, someone else should know the truth about how the AI has taken on her creator's face. Somehow I know this is going to be important in trying to figure out a way to defeat the AI.

I also don't want to be thinking about Raj.

Taking to Skye made me realize that I was secretly hoping I could pull Skye into plans to rescue Raj. I need help, and Skye could help me with a connect to open the Norm's few doors or access pipes. I've been thinking I might be able to get in through the water pipes that we use to drain water from the Norm's storage tanks. The danger in that is if the AI knows I'm there, the AI could flood the pipes and I'd drown.. I don't want to die—not like that.

Blowing out the lamp, I have to wait for my eyes to accustom to the darkness. It's night, and without a moon, the tunnels seem darker than ever. I used to find it comforting, but now the tunnels just feel like a prison. That's part of the reason why I like to go to the Empties— they're open with sky above and space. I hope that Wolf hasn't left on the scavenge, yet—and I also hope he will ask me to come along. But I'm not counting on it.

Wolf's in the space that is sometimes called the Ready Room. It's a storage place. The clan keeps water skins, dried food, pouches, spare parts for the ATs, coats for cold nights, and even some power supply boxes for the ATs.

With his elbows braced on a roughly-hewn stone table, Wolf looks up as I step in. The stone takes up the center of the room, and Wolf is talking with Mole, a short girl, and Komodo, whose bald head gleams in the faint starlight.

I know Wolf knows I'm here, even though I keep to the shadows. His shoulders tense and he glances my way. But when Wolf waves the other two away and turns to see me, I cannot see his expression.

Screwing up my courage, I head over to him, and tell Wolf, "I need to talk to you."

Wolf gives a nod to Mole and Komodo. For a moment, it seems like Komodo might not leave. In the faint light, I can feel tension in the room, but Mole strides out and Komodo follows after her.

Wolf turns to me. Wetting my lips, I ask, "If you find gear will you bring it back?"

"It's not our focus."

I tell him quickly what I learned about the AI—about Conie and Dr. Sig. About how I can read the old language with the biogear. Wolf doesn't move a muscle. I almost want to hit him just to make him react. Instead, I ask, "Don't you have anything to say?"

Wolf lets out a long breath that brushes over my cheek. "Some are nervous about going out. Last scavenge wasn't so good."

"If you want, I'll go," I say. Wolf stands very still, but I tell him, "That's what I wanted to talk to you about anyway. I can go the opposite direction. We can test if drones come after me in biogear and those with me in biogear or after the scavenge teams."

Tension fills the small room. It suddenly seems too crowded, with meat drying on hooks hung on the wall and water skins stacked in one corner, the large stone table and the even larger Wolf who looms in front of me like a huge shadow. Is he going to turn me down? Will he just say the council said no biogear?

"Crow will go with me." Or that is what I hope. "And Alis."

Wolf shakes his head. Even in the dim room, I can see his head move, feel the air move around me from his movement. "You don't have to go on every scavenge. You don't have to make everything about the AI, Lib."

"I don't. But it's what life has made it."

Wolf shifts on his feet. Again, the air seems to move around us. Tension still fills the room, and it leaves me wanting to finger the skins I wear now, or to shuffle a boot into the sand under my feet. I am guessing, but feel certain that Wolf isn't happy about my request. But he has to see the truth in my words—the AI pushed this war on us.

He lets out another sigh and says, the words clipped short, "Make sure the others are willing. I'm not ordering anyone into biogear."

"You don't have to," I tell him.

I turn and walk out. I need to figure out who's still willing to go with me. I hope I am right about Crow being willing to come with me. But is anyone other than Dat and Alis willing to wear biogear?

Chapter Eleven

I end up with a small team of three beside me—Alis, Crow and Dat. Skye seems to be avoiding me. It still hurts that she thinks I'm doing the wrong thing with the biogear. At least Alis is excited.

"It'll give me a chance to test out the modifications on my biogear," she says. She manages to make me feel a little better about what I'm doing here.

I head out to find Crow and ask if he'll come with us. Crow is tall and talks as little as Wolf does. He listens to my request to come out and nods. He touches the scar on his face. Other than that white line, his skin is perfectly smooth. He's thinner than Wolf, but has a sharp nose and I can't help but notice that he's attractive. Dark stubble shades his jaw, and his sun-darkened skin makes the sharp angles of his face seem more interesting. His eyes are large and a mix of gold and green that make him look exotic.

"You disappointed?" Crow asks.

I blink. "About what?" I ask.

He smiles, but only one side of his mouth tips up. "About just going out to be a distraction—a test. No scooping up parts off dead drones." He almost sounds disappointed that we won't be going after the AI's drones.

I bite my lower lip, shrug, and tell him, "I'm really just happy to be going out."

He nods. "Yeah, kind of tired of staying in the dark myself. But you know how the council is. Takes them forever to decide to even think about having cacti for dinner." He winks at me.

I can't help a smile. I've only been out once or twice with Crow, but he's always been easy to work with. We start down the tunnel, heading for the Gear Room. "I have to pick up my biogear." Glancing sideways at Crow I ask, "Do you want to try it on?"

He starts to answer, but turning a corner we find Bird standing in the middle of the tunnel, arms crossed over her chest and frowning.

Bird blocks the way to the Gear Room and she says, voice low and intense, "Leave your gear behind—it's a danger to everyone who touches it."

"Whoa, easy there." Crow holds up his hands and steps between us. "That's strong talk."

Bird doesn't even glance at him. Her stare is fixed on me, her eyes dark and glittering. "You haven't been out there with her. You haven't seen—" She breaks off.

I know instantly that she's talking about the visions that sometimes come to her—the sights of things that might happen.

But I don't really believe anyone can see the future—I think Bird has…dreams of possibilities. I have too many dreams of things I don't want to have happen. "No one's going to get hurt," I tell her, forcing myself to speak slow and soft. "We're only going out to test the biogear."

"And if the drones come after you?"

I shake my head. "We can outrun them. We'll be on ATs. But I don't think we'll see any drones. Not this time. You'll see—the biogear doesn't pull them in."

She turns to Crow. "She's going to get you killed. You and Alis and that kid, Dat. She's more machine than human and you'll pay the price for her being so stubborn about using gear."

Crow lifts a hand. "Then that's my call what I do, isn't it?"

"Bird, it doesn't do either of us any good to keep fighting like this. I know a lot of things are changing, but —"

"This isn't about change," Bird says. "You want us all to be in biogear. Did you ever stop to think maybe that's what the AI wants—all of us to be something she can manipulate. We start wearing bits of gear off drones, we start becoming drones. Where does it stop?"

I reply through gritted teeth, "Gear is just a tool."

Her mouth pulls down. "You're going to destroy everything. I've already seen it."

I step up to face her. "You ever stop to think maybe you saw the AI destroying everything—and only the biogear can change that?"

Her cheeks redden. She drops her arms to the side, turns and walks away, her back stiff.

Glancing at me, Crow says, "What ant got in her britches?"

"She thinks she's right. And I...I don't know how to talk to her anymore."

Crow turns to face me. The scar running down his cheek came from a night cat attack when he was first learning to hunt, or so I heard. He smiles, but part of his face doesn't lift. "Some people don't need talk—they need to see things. Now, you want to show me how that biogear works?"

*   *   *

The biogear doesn't fit Crow and won't work for him. He shrugs off the malfunction, but I am left puzzled. Alis has worked so hard to get the new pack done and it works for her. But the biogear almost seems to have its own mind about who it will connect to and who can't use it.

I have to wonder if there is something in the blood or skin, maybe a conductivity that is at work. Alis and Dat slip on their biogear and fasten their straps. Mine goes on even faster. Crow tells me he'll drive one of the larger ATs. I am not a good driver, but Dat says he can handle a second

AT. He's small, but I believe in him—he is good with anything mechanical.

We head toward the brightest star in the sky. The ATs make a soft humming sound that seems like the wind whistling through the tree branches. Cold wind licks my face. Even though I have been out on my own in my biogear, I keep scanning the sky for drones. I almost want to see a drone on my biogear screen—I want to test out the noise system to see if it blocks drone communication. But it's also nice to just be out without the fear of a drone looking for us.

Heading around the back of the low hills, we make the flatlands, far away from the tunnels. With Dat driving, I have time to think and my mind strays to Wolf. He took Bird out with his team—are they really going to get much water from the plants? We usually don't scavenge for water from the plants unless the wet season has left a lot of them green.

Dat turns the AT, heading for a smooth part of the flatlands. This area almost looks like the paved paths in the Norm or in the Empties. I haven't seen this kind of smoothness before in the Outside. Next to me, Alis rides behind Crow. She, too, keeps scanning the sky, looking for drones with her biogear screen.

Riding on the AT always reminds me of how I used to go out with Raj, back when I was still so new to all of this. It's a strange memory, because it's both painful and comforting. I wouldn't trade it for anything, but thinking of Raj—his scent and how the air would tumble his dark curls —leaves a dull ache in my chest.

I silently vow again to find a way to find out what happened to Raj.

Just as I think that, a structure appears on my biogear screen. It shows power as a white glow. Looking past the screen, I see a platform in the distance. This is a long way away from the Norm, and it is odd to find a platform out in the middle of nowhere like this.

I tap Dat's shoulder and point to the square structure that looks odd against the rolling hills on the horizon. He turns and must see the platform on his biogear screen for he nods and changes direction. Crow follows us now. Not long after that we slow and come to a stop. Swinging off the AT, I glance around.

The platform looks old and half-ruined. It's partially buried by dirt and the roof is smashed. The sides look as if some animal has peeled them back. Dust swirls around us, pulled up from the ground by a strong breeze that pushes at my back.

Alis walks up to me and asks, "Aren't we just testing the biogear?"

I nod, but I also glance around. No drones. Nothing to really use the biogear. In a way this is a test—the biogear hasn't called any drones to us. But why is an access platform out here?

The idea comes to me of how I read there were once many domes—not just one over the Norm. Was there once a dome out here? It seems unlikely, but why else would there be a platform. Did the AI once pull resources from everywhere? It is a chilling thought for it means the AI has been taking water, food, and stripping this world of everything we need to live for a very long time.

Walking onto the steel floor of the platform, I use the biogear screen to check the systems. "There's power," I tell Alis.

Crow calls out from where he sits. "Think you can do a connect?"

"For what?" I ask.

Crow points to a tank that is more than half buried in the sand. "That's a water tank. Or it was. Could be there's still some in it and we've got four empty containers on the ATs."

We do. I glance around. Dat looks eager, ready for anything. He shifts from one booted foot to the other. Alis is watching the sky, checking and rechecking for danger. I like how cautious she is. Crow slumps on his AT as if this is no big deal.

Looking at Alis, I tell her, "We have to be careful, just in case things go wrong with the connect. Let's make it fast. It's one thing for us to get killed out here. It's another for us to bring death home with us."

"How about we don't do either of those things," Dat mutters.

I nod. That's a good plan.

"Dat and Crow, keep an eye out for drones. I'll do the connect with Alis. If anything shows up in the sky, get us out of the connect. Be ready to move fast. We're not here to take on any drones."

But if drones come, I am going to try to block their communications.

Crow frowns and mutters something, but he gives a jerky nod that looks like reluctant agreement. It's obvious he wants to do more than just watch for drones.

Alis is already sizing up the platform and brushing sand off the connect railing. She looks as if she is checking to make sure there is enough power for a connect. I am not really sure we will get any water from the buried tank, but some water is better than none. And a connect will be an even better test of Alis's biogear.

Glancing back, I see Crow standing next to Dat now. Dat's pointing out things he can see with the enhanced vision of the biogear. It seems Crow really is interested, and for the first time in a long time a tingle of hope warms me. If we can get Crow into biogear, that's one more person better able to fight the drones.

But why didn't the biogear work right away with him?

"Ready?" Alis asks.

Turning, I head over to stand next to her. The platform's metal floor is rusted and worn thin in spots. It creaks under my skin boots and light step. Did the AI put this platform out here just because there was deep water it could pull from the ground? We'll soon find out.

Glancing around, I check the sky again. I know I don't need to, but I am remembering my last fight with the drones and how there were so many of them.

No drones, not even the distant whine of one. But there are other dangers out here, too, including animals that hunt in the night and sand storms that can come up in an instant.

Turning to Alis, I ask, "How does it look?"

"Power's low, but should be enough for a connect." She rubs her hands together.

I nod. "Let's get going. I've never been in a connect and had the power go out on me, and I'd rather not try that."

"Right," she says.

Together, we each put a hand on the railing. A familiar prick on my palm tells me I'm linking up. The Outside seems to fade.

Connection: Secure.

The connection is not secure. The virtual world wobbles around me, unsteady, tipping to one side and then the other, fading and then snapping into sharp focus. All the spinning leaves my stomach doing flips. I have to swallow down bile that stings my throat. I glance to my left. Alis stands with her hands out to her sides as if struggling to stay balanced. The colors swirl around us.

Putting a hand on her shoulder, I ask, "You good, or do you need to get out?"

She swallows several times. Her virtual appearance is pale and shimmering, but she manages to straighten. "I'm good."

I nod. Reaching out, I wave and think about access. It takes longer than it should but a screen appears before me, showing lines of code that scroll past. The biogear screen lets me read the code faster than I have before. The code scrolls past in jerky fits and starts. Thinking about water, I start my search, but the rattling code makes my head ache.

I can feel Alis watching me and she edges closer as if she's either fascinated or needs me to help steady her.

Connects work differently for me than for anyone else. Rogues can't really connect—not even with biogear. They need a Glitch, a former Tech, to get access into the AI's systems. But I can access the systems with just a thought—hacking the system seems to come naturally to me.

I don't think much about what I do—the virtual world just changes for me.

It would be nice to think this is only a natural gift, but I fear it's really the result of the AI tampering with me. The AI made me special, and I want to use that against her.

I have to hope the AI will not be able to turn this ability against me instead.

Ignoring Alis's watchful gaze, I scan the code, looking for right lines that can unlock water access. If there's water in the storage tank, we'll have to hope that opening the pipes won't dump the water into the ground below us—the pipes might be buried.

The world flutters again, and I tell Alis, "See if you can find the power source and stabilize it with the power source box off your biogear. Just don't let the system drain your biogear. I don't know what might happen to you in the AI's virtual world if that happens.

Alis nods. "On it."

She moves away and finds a power connect. It takes her a few heartbeats to finally connect her biogear into the platform's system. For a moment, the virtual world dims and I am both standing on the platform with Alis and within the cool blue of the AI's systems. Then the virtual world brightens and steadies.

Glancing back at the screen, I find the lines of code to open the water storage tank in the real world. I open water access and hope Dat and Crow are ready with the water storage tanks to get the water.

I start to close the screen, but the code flickers and new lines appear. This code is different from any other I have ever seen—it seems to have some of the old language embedded. It is not just machine code.

I blink several times and touch a fingertip to one line.

The screen shimmers and shifts. The code vanishes. Images appear, but not static ones like those I found in the Empties.

These images move.

I'm fascinated. The images show a group of people with rain coming down on them—lots of rain. I almost start to smile, but there's something wrong. The images jerk and almost flicker out, but come back and I can see the expressions on the people's faces—they're terrified. Panicking. They press close to each other as if being shoved together.

Then I see the wall.

The wall is huge and smooth and seems to rise up forever. The people press against the wall, water at their feet and rising higher. I have never seen so much water. This should be a good thing, but it is terrifying. The people in the image trample one another. People go down, splashing into the water and never coming up again. Some are crying, others screaming without making any sound, just with open mouths and hair plastered to their heads and their clothes dragged down by so much water. My heart is pounding and I almost don't want to watch, but I must.

The water keeps pouring down, and I realize the wall is really part of the Norm—it's the wall of the dome around the Norm.

But why is it raining so much?

The storm seems to get worse for the video darkens and blurs. There is no sound, but the images blank out and I am left staring at a black blur.

With a hollow pit in my stomach I know these people are long ago dead. I have never seen clothes such as they wore—for they didn't wear skins and didn't wear tunics. There are no more flooding rains—not unless the AI makes them. I have seen the weather program the AI can manipulate and I have to wonder if the AI caused the rain to kill all these people.

Alis's voice startles me. "We done?" There is a strain in her voice when she calls out to me. I glance at her and see her virtual form is wavering—her biogear's power low light is on. I wipe out the screen and tell her, "Let's get out of here."

Chapter Twelve

Coming out of the connect leaves me blinking and breathing hard. The splash of water and whoops from Dat tell me the water tank pipes opened—the hack of the water storage system worked. I smell dampness in the air.

Dat and Crow scavenge three containers of water—the metal containers are old, salvaged long ago from the Empties. They're the clan's most precious good. Crow is smiling. He and Dat lash the water containers onto the back of the ATs with thick ropes made of dried plants. We have one container left empty, but three is better than none.

In the distance, lightning strikes, brightening the sky.

Glance at the sky, I worry a storm might be coming. Storms blow in fast, bringing stinging sand. The sky is just starting pale with dawn coming and the early light paints red across clouds. Will they bring us rain?

I keep thinking about all those people I saw in the moving images and all that rain—why did the AI kill them? Or did she? Did the rain just come on its own, pounding and unstoppable? Was that another reason to build the

Norm, to keep the rain from killing everyone? But then why didn't the AI let those people into the Norm?

I'm left with even more questions than I had. That's happening all too often. I also have to wonder how I could access those moving images. Did the AI want me to see them, or did the code to access the images show up only because the platform was old and failing?

Calling information requires concentration—so it seems unlikely I would have asked for moving images. I've never seen them before. Never that I remember. I am almost certain someone else triggered the access. But would the AI do that?

Thinking about this, I decide the AI is far too clever— she would only show me the moving images if it was part of a plan. This means the moving images must be connected either to her desire to destroy the Rogues and Glitches, or it is connected to her desire to leave this world with the Norm.

Or I really did access it because of something buried in my memories and without the AI knowing it.

This last idea leaves me shaken. The AI is growing all the time—she told me that herself. Growth is a sign of life, and the AI is alive, even if she is a machine. But how much has she grown? Has she been around so long that she has old systems she no longer monitors—systems she may not even be aware she has because they are old and she thinks she has outgrown them? This seems possible. She leaves sentinels—firewalls—to guard water and other supplies. We wouldn't be able to access them if the AI was really watching everything.

This idea stirs hope that I can get back into the Norm without the AI knowing—maybe by using old systems she no longer cares about. I am starting to think that coupled with the work I have been doing to make the biogear send out communication noise will work to get me into the Norm. But I still must find Raj's location.

I have the ride back to the tunnels to think about all of this, but I come back to the same idea—my answers are all to be found in the Norm. This gives me even more reason to get back inside—it's not just that I must find Raj. I must find out why the AI keeps trying to use me. And I must find out how to stop her.

We leave the ATs hidden, covered up and tucked under a rock overhang. This means we have to carry the water to the tunnels. Crow takes one container, Dat and Alis take one and I have to carry the third. It seems to grow heavier with every step. I am left sweating and out of breath, my arms shaking from the effort.

It is past dawn when we return with water. Gazelle and Wolf greets us in the tunnels. Wolf seems surprised at the water, but pleased. He tells me the other scavenge groups came back with a few plants and not much more. We need rains to come, but I am uneasy about that now after seeing the moving images of how too much rain is bad.

I don't see Bird, and that is a relief.

Wolf takes the water container from me and carries it to storage. I take Dat's place with Alis and help her lug the water, following behind Wolf and Crow—they make it look easy.

Once we have the containers poured into the larger, stone cisterns that hold our water supply, Crow turns to me and says, "You ever head out again, let me know. And we can try that biogear again."

With a smile, Crow takes the empty containers with him to store back on the ATs. Wolf is frowning at me now. "Biogear?" he asks. "For Crow?"

I make a noncommittal sound. Wolf shakes his head and walks away. I'm left frowning after him. Is Wolf going to ask me to stop making biogear for others?

Coming up to me, Alis nudges my arm with her elbow. "That Crow's not half bad."

I glance at her and tell her, "Let's see if we can't figure out why the biogear didn't work on him."

We spend most of the day adjusting the new biogear pack, but there is no reason why it shouldn't work on Crow —it works on me, on Alis and on Dat. This leaves me convinced the bio component of the gear must be unique to each person, but I don't know what to do with that information.

Dat grows bored as Alis and I take apart the biogear pack one more time. He starts tinkering with some gear, using wire and drone parts to make something about the size of a biogear pack, but it has legs and arms and a round, red light that flickers. It looks too much like a small drone.

Shivers race down my spine. I look away from it.

Since Dat is absorbed with tinkering on something, I lean closer to Alis. I keep my voice low. This is not something I want Dat to hear. What I'm planning is risky, and Dat is still so very young. I want to try to protect him if I can, but I need help.

Picking up a coil of wire, I ask Alis, "Have you ever thought about going back to the Norm?"

Alis straightens with a sharp move and stares at me, eyes wide and her eyebrows flying high. "Go back to what? The AI threw me out—one mistake in code and I was tossed like I was old bones. Besides, there's no way back into the Norm that I know of—the door I was tossed out of shut tight behind me with no way to open it again."

"I know, but have you *thought* about it?"

She frowns and rubs the back of her hand with one finger. Dirt from the scavenge streaks the back of her hand. She pushes a strand of reddish hair away from her face, glances at Dat and then says, her voice soft, "It's hard not to. The Norm was once all I knew. You never forget that." Her face flushes red. "Sorry, I mean, most of us don't forget—not unless we're wiped by the AI before we're tossed out because we knew too much about her systems."

I wave her off like it's not a big deal, but of course it is. I once thought I was a Glitch who had a memory wipe. But at times I wonder if I ever had any memories to wipe. "I understand." I glance over at Dat. He has pulled the arms off the thing he is building and now watches as they flop on the dirt floor. Turing back to Alis, I say, "You didn't know Raj, did you? I mean, you didn't know him in the Outside. You came to us after we lost Raj, but…did you ever know him in the Norm?"

Lips pressed tight, eyes narrowed, she thinks about it and then shakes her head. "Not that I can recall. The Norm is a big place and a Tech is supposed to stay put, do the work and be happy. Anything else gets you thrown out."

"I know Skye was deemed a Glitch because she had these fits—seizures. The AI hates flaws like that."

Alis nods. "That's not all she hates." She pokes at a loose wire on the biogear. "Like I said, a Tech is supposed to do the work. You keep to your own group and…well, even picking a partner match is supposed to be handled by the AI with genetic matching."

I frown. "What if you don't like a match?"

"There's no choice. And you can't go against the AI—the AI always finds out about every little thing you do." Alis lifts a hand. "The system makes sense in a way. The Norm has limited resources. It's not as bad as Outside, but Techs have only limited food options, even more limited choices about where to live, and you'd be surprised how many repairs have to be handled with recycled parts. All that means the AI has to limit the number of Techs in the Norm—so there is a limit on who you can be with or not."

"But she also…throws people away. That's wrong. Choice should be something that matters. Even the Rogue clans know that much."

With a weak smile, she leans against the stone wall. "I don't know. I don't see anyone here making great choices. Sure, choice is good, but what if you can't make a good choice? What if you never find someone because of that? Or even worse, what if you find someone and end up producing unhealthy offspring. I'd hate that."

"How do you know so much about all this?"

She looks away. Tension holds her still and her shoulders hunch slightly. "It's not like any of that was a secret," she mumbles. "But…well, my area…I was a Tech in genetics. That was kind of what I did—reviewed the genetic database and proofed the algorithms."

"You paired people?"

"No. The AI handled that. But I reviewed compatibilities. It was data streams with potentiality. I had to adjust for changing conditions."

"And you changed something you shouldn't have?"

Pushing off the wall, she turns back to the gear. "I tried to tweak the algorithm. My brother…he liked this Tech who was younger than him. She wasn't his match. I adjusted the code. The AI found out—I think another Tech informed on me—and I was thrown out. I…I don't know what happened to my brother. Maybe he's okay with the match the AI made for him."

"Happy? Does the AI allow that? Or even care? She just gets rid of anything that doesn't conform. She throws

Glitches out figuring everyone will die in the Outside and she sends drones out to kill the Rogues."

Alis sighs. "I know. But…I'm not sure the AI hates us. The AI just…just is."

I picture the Norm as I saw it when I hacked a way inside with Raj—green plans, pretty buildings, smiling Techs.

And then those smiles froze, the AI took control of the Techs and tried to have those people kill Raj. We barely escaped. But then Raj was trapped and I was almost killed by Conie.

It's hard for me to think of the Techs as beings capable of happiness or any other emotion. Perhaps the AI has made every Tech into something that is part machine. Cold slips down my back. Maybe Bird has a point about the dangers of mixing gear into someone's body—maybe for a Rogue it is a danger. The Rogues are born in the Outside—but the rest of us who come from the Norm are something other than just human.

Staring at my hand, I open and close my fingers. Then I look at Alis. "I need to go back to the Norm. Will you help me?"

Alis glances over at Dat. He is absorbed in taking apart the thing he built, turning it back into parts. She shakes her head and says, "Didn't you try that? I mean, I know I was kicked out of the Norm after everything else, but I've heard the stories from others. You went back inside—hacked into the Norm. But you almost died. That's what the others say. Why would you want to go back for more of that?"

"I wasn't the only one back inside."

"Raj." Alis's voice is soft.

I nod. "If you heard the talk about me, you heard the talk about him, too."

She looks away, but her glance slides back to me. "I have. You and Raj went into the Norm. You got out. He didn't."

"Raj wanted to…to fix the AI. But the AI—Conie—was a lot smarter and more dangerous than we expected. But I keep thinking about Raj. I have to go back and see if he is still alive. Not only that, but the AI really is going to try and take the Norm away from this world. If she does, we're all dead. I kept hoping I would find out something through the drones, but the AI is too smart for that. I've got some ideas on how to get back in, and the last time I didn't have biogear. That's going to make a difference. But I don't think I can do this on my own—and succeed."

Alis twirls a strand of hair around one finger and tips her head to the side. "This is a crazy idea, but crazy can work. Do you think you can get Wolf to agree to it? I mean, seems like the council is all about being really cautious and Wolf is all about doing right by what the council says. I heard he also was there when you barely got out of the Norm."

"It doesn't matter what Wolf or the Council thinks. I'm not going to tell him or them. This is something I have to do, and Wolf is needed by the clan. I can't let him risk himself over this."

Alis's eyes brighten "Sounds like you've thought about that part of it. But are you really going to try this with just two of us? And what about supplies? Anyone doing anything in the Outside needs water and food, and we're going to need more than just the idea of hacking into the Norm."

"I've been thinking about all of this. Going out on a scavenge isn't going to make anyone worry. We go out with what we need—and who we need."

She frowns. "Who? You're hoping it's more than just you and me?"

"Crow will go with us. I think Tiger will, too, if we can get him back into biogear. I don't want to take Dat—he's so young. But I'm thinking maybe Otter is ready for some payback for Sidewinder's death. That's about all I want going with us. We'll be better off if we can get everyone into biogear. I have some ideas about how to hide us from the drones."

Alis wets her lips, glances at Dat, and then back to me. "What if someone finds out what we're planning—and by someone I mean Wolf?"

"Then I'll have to explain myself to him. Until then, we keep it a secret. Even if you don't want to come with me— and that's a choice you can make—will you promise not to tell anyone what I am planning?"

For a second she chews on her lower lip. She lets out a breath and waves a hand. "I don't know. Wolf's clan leader, if he finds out…they could throw us out. How long do you think we can survive in the Outside without a clan?"

I almost want to laugh. "Alis, the AI isn't going to let any of us live. Now, we can die down here in the tunnels, pretending nothing's going to change. Or we can try to fight the AI and stop her. I'd rather die fighting for my life —for the lives of others—and not just pretend I don't know better."

"You really think the AI is going to leave? I heard…I've heard others say you're the only one who heard the AI say this. Are you really sure the AI wasn't lying?"

"Alis, you've been in a connect. You've hacked the AI systems—you know how the AI thinks. Are you going to tell me you can't believe the AI isn't trying to stockpile resources and make the Norm self-sufficient?"

She frowns. "When you put it like that…it makes sense. The Norm…when I was little, it seemed like there was more. More food. More water. There's been less and less until it was just enough to get by on." She straightens. "When are we doing this?"

"Soon. First we need some plans and I need to find the best access point into the Norm."

*   *   *

It takes two days before I have a chance to ask Crow if he is interested in going on a different kind of scavenge—one that means hitting the Norm directly.

He offers up a crooked grin and a nod and tells me, "Just let me know when." He gives me a wink and walks away. It feels odd to share a secret with him and it feels strangely intimate.

After I ask Crow, I head over to talk to Otter. He has not been eating much and has been moody ever since the death of his brother. When I ask if he wants a chance to avenge Sidewinder, Otter's eyes brighten for the first time in far too long. He gives me a nod.

"You'll have to wear biogear," I tell him.

"Just make sure I get to take down drones," he answers.

I go to ask Tiger as well, but he gives me a hard stare and when I ask if he'd like to try on biogear, he walks away. That means he is out. I don't tell him anything more and leave him to his own thoughts.

Alis says I should ask Pike, a girl who has been asking Alis about the gear and who paints designs on the clan's skin with dyes made from plans. I let Alis talk to Pike and she comes to try on the biogear. The pack lights up for her at once—and Pike seems more excited about this than either of us.

Star, a skinny girl with short hair and a hard face, comes to me to tell me she heard from Crow I'm planning to attack the AI. I bite down on the inside of my cheek, but Star says, "There is only one thing I want—the AI gone. You're after that, so I'm with you." She turns and starts to walk away, but glances back and says, "Hawk's with me on this."

Hawk is a short, heavy-set man who is partners with Star. I am surprised to hear he will use biogear. He is the opposite of Star, but when he comes to get a biogear pack, it is clear he wants to be where the action is.

We still need biogear that works on Crow, and as we work on that Alis asks me, "We're really not going to ask Skye to help?"

"No, we're really not."

"But...Skye. I know Dat's too young, but Skye's not. And she's done more connects and hacks than anyone."

"That's the problem. Haven't you seen her on a hack? She hates to connect...hates it. It scares her. This is going to scare her even more. And then she's going to tell Bird and Bird will tell Wolf, and the whole thing is going to become something the council has to talk about it. We've wasted too much time as it is."

Alis opens her mouth as if she's about to argue with me, so I cut her off. "It's not fair to ask her to have to choose between being loyal to Bird or staying silent about this. We have to respect that. We're not going to start acting like the AI and telling people what they have to do—this is about free choice. And I'm not going to ask her to have to make that kind of choice"

Alis shuts her mouth tight, nods and turns away. She seems disappointed, but I think she understands.

Three days later, we have Crow's biogear ready for a trial run. I ask Wolf for permission to head out on a scavenge. He seems reluctant but when I point out that I went out with biogear and got water on the last scavenge, he nods and tells me to be safe. He puts a hand on my shoulder.

For a moment, I want to tell him everything. He helped me escape the Norm the last time I barely got out—he saved my life. I owe him so much. But, much like with Skye and forcing her to choose between fighting the AI and loyalty to Bird, I cannot force a choice on Wolf. I cannot make him have to decide between what he thinks he must do for the good of the clan and what I must do for the good of this entire world.

I turn from Wolf and his hand falls from my shoulder.

Heading to the Gear Room, I find Alis helping Crow into his biogear. Dat sits in a corner, his face pulled into a sulk. "Dat should go."

I glance at him and tell him, "Maybe next time."

He gets up and stomps out. Glancing around, I see Star and Hawk have their biogear on. Star is already able to show Hawk how to work the screen—she seems a fast learner. Pike is helping Otter fasten his straps, but Otter is asking about weapons and how to activate them. I am glad I've given him a biogear pack without weapons for this scavenge.

Looking around the Gear Room, I tell everyone, "Tonight, it's about data collection." Otter looks disappointed as I outline the plan. We're going to the Norm in biogear only—no ATs. "Everyone needs to get used to their biogear—you want to find out how fast you can run, how quick you can move. Test your strength—the biogear works differently for every person."

"Okay, so we're testing," Crow says. He wiggles a little and adjusts his biogear. "But what else are we doing?

I smile at him. "It's time we see what the AI is doing."

Chapter Thirteen

Crow's biogear works fine, but Otter has trouble with his. We have to stop and Alis makes a few adjustments, then we are all running again. Star and Hawk match strides, but Pike is breathing hard by the time we reach the ridge that overlooks the Norm.

We stop behind three large boulders that hide us from view. Alis works on Otter's biogear again—the screen isn't working. I ask Crow and Hawk to keep watch. Pike and Star come over to where I stand.

Peering over the top of the boulders, I use the biogear screen to be able to see with just starlight. A warm wind blows sand across the land, but the night is clear and the stars sharp. Below us, the Norm seems a huge, dark blot on the land. We are high enough up to see the smaller platforms around the dome, and the curving height of the huge walls.

Along the dome wall of the Norm, black drones hover, just floating and watching as if on guard. Their blinking red lights sweep the ground. They seem to be scanning every platform.

"What are they doing?" Pike asks, her voice a soft whisper.

I shake my head. "I'm not entirely sure."

Pike adjusts the screen for her biogear. "There's something else out there."

I adjust my screen to magnify the view. Behind the drones, I glimpse things—machines—scabs. They look almost human—they have arms at least. Six of them. And skeletal bodies and oval heads that don't seem to have faces. At first, it seems as if they are tearing open a wall, but after several moments of watching them, I can see they close it again."

"Are they rewiring something?" Star asks. "Making repairs?"

Glancing at her, I see she has one eye closed and her screen set to maximum view. I do the same and now I can see they do seem to be opening sections of the wall, working on the wiring and then closing the wall again.

Scabs.

The word pops into my mind, a hazy memory. Techs use scabs for outside work on the Norm.

The scabs seem to be changing some kind of functionality. My skin chills and my mouth dries. It seems obvious now—the Norm is built for this world, not to travel in space. Wiring will have to be adjusted to reticulate air instead of just filtering in air from this world. There may be greater power requirements as well—and a need to reuse and recycle waste products since resources will be limited away from this world.

She's really doing it.

One of the scabs works with what looks like thick copper wiring, weaving it into the panel that's been pried open from the wall. "Pike, count the number of drones. See if they do anything other than guard. Star, you're on the scabs."

She glances at me. "The what? You mean those spider-things?"

"Yes, those. It seems like they're working only on certain areas. We need to know what they're doing, but it's going to be hard to find out."

"What am I doing?" Otter asks.

I glance over at him and tell him, "Come with me. You too, Crow. We're going to do a circuit around the Norm. Let's see how the biogear holds up to a long run. Alis, stay here with Pike, Hawk and Star."

Crow, Otter and I head out, picking a careful path down the ridgeline. I don't want to be spotted by the drones, so we stay a long way away from the dome. That means we have an even longer run than if we were close. I tell Crow and Otter to pace themselves. Crow gives me his crooked smile. Otter just nods, his mouth set into a line.

The run leaves me breathing hard, and it soon is obvious that it is impossible for us to run around the entire dome— it's bigger than I thought it would be. We run until the sky begins to lighten. We have to turn back then, and I doubt we have even gone half way around the Norm.

I turn back, but Otter puts a hand out. "I'll go on."

I shake my head. "Can't risk it. We keep seeing drones and scabs working on the wall—it's clear the AI's doing major work. If the drones see you, you're toast. And that'll alert the AI that we're watching her."

Otter frowns, but he follows as I head back. Crow follows as well.

When we reach the others, Star and Pike give me their counts—two hundred drones and fifty scabs. Added to the ones we saw, that makes an army of drones and scabs. Far more than we can ever fight. I haven't had a chance to try out the communication noise to see if that will hide us— but now is not the time for that, either. For now, we need to go back.

We slip down off the ridgeline, moving fast. I worry that our boots are kicking up too much dust, but a wind comes up—thankfully—blowing sand that hides our tracks.

Everyone's breathing hard and sweating by the time we make it back to the tunnels. The sun is up and baking all of us. Sweat slicks my back and trickles down between my breasts and sticks my skin trousers to my legs. My boots feel as if they're full of water. Our water skins our empty, so are the pouches we took out to make this look like a scavenge. But I've come back before from a scavenge with little to show for the effort.

At the tunnels I have the others slip down the entrance rope before I go inside. I do a last scan for any drones to make certain we weren't followed, and then I slide down the rope, burning my palms. I'm still not as good at this as the Rogues.

In the tunnels, I have to wait for my eyes to adjust from the bright sunlight to the dim light. The sun beats down through the entrance hole. Instead of Gazelle or someone else from the clan being on watch, Wolf steps in front of me. He glances at my empty pouch, hanging limp by my hip. "Gone a long time," he tells me, accusation in his tone. His large arms are crossed over his chest and he fixes an intense stare on me.

Shoving down the quick kick of panic in my chest, I shrug. "It takes what it takes. You know that. Didn't get anything much, either. The AI's getting tighter on security —connects are harder."

That, at least, is the truth. Connects have gotten harder, and so have the hacks. The AI is hording more and more of the resources we need to survive.

Wolf shakes his head. "Lib—"

"Wolf, either you trust me, or you don't. And if you don't, throw me out."

He says nothing, but the look in his eyes leaves me having to turn away.

I know I am doing the right thing—but that doesn't mean it's easy for me. And I just wish I could trust Wolf more, too.

Resisting the urge to look back at Wolf, I hurry down the tunnel. I don't hear the soft tread of his steps, but I am also certain that Wolf knows I'm doing things he won't like. And that in his own way he is trying to look out for me.

Strangely, that stings. I can look after myself—or that's what I want to believe. The urge to let him do more—to want him to do more for me—is strong. I have to ignore that. I have to remember there is more at stake than whatever is between me and Wolf—the whole world is at risk right now.

In the main room, Crow and Otter are stripping off their biogear and heading for a meal. I grab Otter's biogear—it still needs work. Relief sweeps through me to be back in the tunnels, but I'm worried about what we've seen.

The AI is moving fast—how long will it take her to retrofit the Norm for space travel? And is there anything we can do to delay her?

Those thoughts keep me distracted as I head for the Gear Room. I should get some sleep—I need it. But I am too wound up to rest. Maybe that's part of what the biogear does. Even though I've been up and running, I feel as if I could keep going for hours yet.

I almost run into Skye before I see her. I slow my steps. Skye's blonde hair is down and loose and she plays with the ends of it in a nervous habit. Bird walks next to Skye, small and dark, only her colorful ribbons making her stand out in the dark tunnel.

I slow my steps. I don't really want to talk to Bird right now. I need to think and make plans.

But Bird turns as if she senses me behind her. Her eyes catch mine and our stares lock. Her gaze shifts over to my biogear and she narrows her eyes as if she can't stand to see anyone in biogear. I can practically feel her anger almost like a blaze of heat from the fire in the main room.

Staring back at her, I lift my chin slightly. I won't let her intimidate me.

Bird lets out a huff of air and abruptly turns and walks away, leaving Skye standing alone in the tunnel. Skye turns and glances at me. For a second, her expression is blank—unreadable. Then she offers me a smile and lifts her hand in a small wave. I give her a nod. Her smile drops away as if she doesn't know what to do with it, and she hurries off after Bird.

The whole encounter leaves me…uneasy. It's not that I don't like Bird and Skye being friends. That's their business. But now Bird has seen I have not given up my biogear—she'll soon know that others are wearing biogear, too. That may mean trouble.

Now I have not just the time until the AI tries to take the Norm from this world—I have only so much time until

Bird tries to turn the council against all biogear. That thought leaves a hard knot in my chest. I wish Bird understood better—or that Wolf did. Or that others had actually heard the AI talk of her plans to leave.

But wishing doesn't help anything. I have learned that lesson.

Forcing myself to move, I keep my head down and keep my steps fast.

The Gear Room is empty.

Stripping off my biogear, I miss it almost at once. In the biogear, I feel stronger…I am stronger. It hugs me close. It is like a second skin to me, and the warmth of it against my back seems comforting. I resist the urge to put it on again. I have work to do.

I settle down with Otter's biogear, and start tinkering, but I also start to yawn. I should go and sleep, but I don't want to face Bird and Skye in the tunnels. I don't want to see Wolf's frowns. I just want to put my head down for a minute.

Just a minute.

A clicking noise rattles like stones in a drinking jar. A hiss sounds.

I stare into a face—a smiling, familiar face. The woman seems kind with eyes that seem to say she knows far more than anyone else and will not use such knowledge in the wrong ways. I know her, but...from where?

Her voice seems to echo in memory. Her lips move and form words. But I only catch a few sounds.

Lib...Done...Return.

I shiver, chilled. I know who she is. She is Dr. Sig... Constance. She is the face worn by the AI.

Why are you linked like this?

The question pops into mind, but my lips won't move. I find myself reaching for her. I want answers. She has them. She knows more than anyone else. I can't shake the feeling that she wants me to know what the answers are.

Fear slides into me, slips over my skin. I'm afraid she'll disappear at any moment. Don't leave with my answers. I want to tell her that but nothing comes out of my mouth. I reach for her...

"What are you doing?"

Dat's voice jerks me awake and I sit up and blink.

Dr. Sig is gone. Or was that Conie?

Putting a hand to my head, I find my hair is matted and I've been slumped over the work area. Otter's biogear screen feels like it is printed onto my cheek. My mouth is dry and the fragments of the dream cling to me like dust from the Outside.

Leaning over me, Dat frowns, his eyebrows flat and tight and his eyes filled with uncertainly.

"I'm…" I let the words trail off.

Dreaming? That isn't the right word for what happened. It was more like…like a vision. I don't know if this is a memory trying to surface, or if the AI can somehow connect to my mind in that stage between rest and full awareness.

How could anyone else understand what happens to me when I don't understand it?

"Nothing," I tell him. "I fell asleep."

His eyebrows dart high and he rubs a hand into his pale hair which is sticking up. "You looked like you were going to activate the biogear communications—in your sleep."

Now I frown. That doesn't sound good. Turning away, I glance at Otter's biogear. Somehow I seemed to have put it back together. I touch the screen. "I was dreaming about a woman. Someone important."

"Someone I know?" he asks.

"I don't think so."

He heads over to his corner where he has been tinkering again with gear, building something that looks like a box with lights. Squatting down next to the black box, he says, "Bird says dreams matter. Wind says that, too. Tracker Clan doesn't have much use for dreams, but the Sees Far Clan, they all dream. And they have a dream weaver—at least Bird says they do. The weaver can give you good dreams...ones that help you make sense of what's really in your head."

I glance over to where he sits and stares at his box. "Do you talk a lot with Bird?" I ask.

He shakes his head and wrinkles his nose. "No. Bird talks at me. She always wants to know what I've been dreaming. She and Wind are both always poking into everyone's dreams." He glances up at me. "You must dream a lot, too."

"What do you mean?"

"I mean…well, everyone knows you got wiped. Wind says that a Glitch that's been wiped isn't really wiped—she says things can't just be gone. So that means your memories have to have been moved. Hidden. So they can only show up in dreams while you're sleeping."

"That actually makes a lot of sense."

He shrugs. "I know. I hate it when Bird and Wind are always right. They never let you forget it."

I have to smile. "I do know what that's like."

Grinning, he runs his hand through his hair in a gesture I am certain he learned from Wolf. After a moment he says, "Maybe she's your mom."

I freeze. I have no family I can remember. But I must have come from somewhere.

Dat lets out a long sigh. "I don't remember my mom, either. Or a father. I must have had one. Maybe a brother or a sister, too. But...I don't think I was wiped. They just aren't in memory. Skye says I was put Outside too young to remember. Or that I was put Outside the Norm because my memory is bad—faulty." In a soft voice, he adds, "I really hate the AI."

I know what to say. My throat is tight. I didn't know before now how much Dat hates the AI, but I can see it in his eyes, in the taut line of his back, in how his fists clench around a copper wire.

He forces his hand open and smooths the bent wire.

"No one's going to force you away from the Tracker Clan," I tell him.

He glances up at me, his face still for a moment. Then he smiles. "Doesn't matter if they do. I have you."

Those simple words shake me. He has me—me? I have never before thought that anyone had ties to me, but Dat does. Does Wolf? And Skye? Is this why they worry so much about my using biogear—they have me?

Dat bends over his box again, fiddling with the wires to change the light sequencing several times.

A voice calls out to Dat from the tunnels—one of the other young men from the clan wanting Dat to come with them to try and catch snakes or rabbits for dinner. I frown.

A boy pushes into the entrance to the Gear Room. It's Dog. His skin dark from the sun, his hair curly and wild. "Come on, Dat."

I glance at Dat and see worry, eagerness and loneliness cross his face in rapid expressions.

Standing, I walk over and nudge Dat's shoulder. "Go on. We could use some fresh meat tonight."

Dat grins, stands and hurries off with Dog. But Dat stops in the doorway and tells me, "You should ask Bird for help with those dreams. She helped Skye."

Dat heads off and I am left staring at the biogear and thinking about Dat's words.

Asking Bird for help seems the opposite of what I need to do—but Bird does know about dreams. And I need to know if these are dreams, or if the AI is contacting me somehow. If she is, then I am a huge danger to the clan, and I can't allow that. I can't let the AI know anything we're planning.

Standing, I stretch and then search for Skye.

I find Skye in the women's sleeping area, sitting on a thick sheepskin and braiding Bird's hair.

Habit makes me hesitate, but I walk over to them and force a smile. "I need to talk about a dream, Bird."

The words come out blunt and rough and nothing like what I'd wanted them to be.

Skye smiles as if she thinks I'm funny. Bird tips her head to one side. She doesn't seem angry—more like relieved. Maybe because I don't have biogear on?

Waving at me to sit down, Skye says, "We were just about to come see you."

My mouth falls open a little. I want to step back but instead I cross my arms and then let my hands fall back to my sides. "You were?" I clear my throat and say a little stronger. "You were…why?"

Skye waves again to the skins. She turns back to finish a braid on Bird's thick, dark hair. "Wolf told Bird about you going to the Empties on your own… and Bird knows how to help you find what you're searching for."

Chapter Fourteen

How could Bird possibly know about anything that I need?

For a moment, I'm ready to turn and walk away, but Bird is looking at me with a mixture of challenge and curiosity in her eyes, as if she wants to see what I will do. I'm curious as well—and I keep remembering what Dat said about Bird knowing about dreams. And Bird once asked me why I dream of death. I want to get back to a place where Bird is more of an ally—maybe this is the way. I glance at Skye.

She smiles and stands. "Come with us."

Bird gets to her feet as well with an ease I have never known. Bird leads the way, Skye follows her, and I trail after them. A mixture of anticipation and dread churns in my stomach. Is this really smart? What if Bird is just playing a game with me? What if this is just their idea of mocking me?

Skye seems to sense my hesitation for she glances back and motions for me to keep up with her. We walk back to the main room and cross it, then take one of the smaller tunnels that I've never used—I've never needed to use it.

There are always fast-exit tunnels off the main room. They're smaller than the other tunnels we use and they only matter if the tunnels are ever attacked. Because they aren't used much, they tend to end up with spider webs in the corners and sometimes with small animals living inside them.

This tunnel is tiny—narrow and so low I have to stoop. I almost wish for a lamp because it is also black. I can see nothing. I have to feel my way with a hand to each wall and listen for Skye and Bird's soft footsteps.

The escape tunnel winds and twists in ways the other main tunnels don't. This is typical for an escape route—the idea is that any drone trying to track you down a tunnel like this won't be able to get a clean shot. It will have to come after anyone fleeing and may smash into a wall if it's going so fast it can't make one of the tight turns. That also means these small, twisting tunnels are a great way to pull any invading drone away from the clan.

My back starts to cramp from my having to bend over and walk. This tunnel seems to go on forever, but that is due to the darkness. I lose track of the number of turns. Every now and then the tunnel branches and Skye tells me to go right or left. I start to worry I will never find my way back to the main room. But any exit tunnel has to have an exit somewhere.

Hurrying to keep up with Skye, I want to tell her that she almost doesn't seem like her normal self. She is never as quiet as this. It makes me wonder if there's a lot about Skye I don't know.

Bird just strides ahead of us, her boot steps soft and firm and the faint whisper of the ribbons on her clothes and hair stirring the air. She seems to know where she is going.

After what seems like forever, the tunnel finally opens up into a room and I can stand straight again. Fist-sized holes in the ceiling let the golden light of sunset into the room. It is later than I thought it would be—I slept longer than I knew in the Gear Room.

This light glints off pale walls that seem to sparkle with some kind of reflecting mineral or crystal, and the sand is pale and white as well. Skye heads to the center of the room, leans over a circle of stones and soon has a fire going with flint and a metal striker.

Oddly, three other tunnels branch out from this room, which seems odd for an escape route. Heading over to one of the white walls, I see that carvings have been etched into the stone—just rough marks that look like a drawing of the Empties.

Other carvings show rough stick figures holding hands.

I walk over to a hide that is stretched on a frame. More drawings are here—and the hide looks very old. The drawings are better here—more accurate. Someone has used plant dye to sketch old people holding long sticks that seem to grow into trees on one end, branching out and then bearing fruit. The trees keep reaching up to the stars, up into a night sky.

I have no idea what the painting on the skin is supposed to mean. Turning, I glance around, looking for Bird and Skye.

Bird sits next to the fire, cross-legged on the white sand, the orange flame sending dancing shadows over her face and her small frame. Light filters down on her through one of the holes in the ceiling. Skye sits opposite Bird, also cross-legged and underneath another of the ceiling holes. Skye waves for me to sit between her and Bird, to one side of the fire.

There's no stone to sit on. No fur or hide.

Bird pulls off her boots and Skye does the same, so I sit down and take off my boots as well.

Leaning forward, Bird takes up a wooden bowl that was nestled between the rocks of the fire ring. She dips her fingers into the bowl and they come out with white fluid dripping off her fingertips. Bird paints her cheeks with three white lines on each side. She brushes her fingers into the sand to clean them and hands me the bowl. But I just keep watching her.

Taking up a stick from the fire that has a cold, burnt end, Bird touches the stick to a finger and then smudges the black soot around her eyes and down each hand with one finger. She turns and stares at me, her eyes seeming huge now with the black lines around them.

I copy her, since that seems to be what Bird wants me do to, smearing white lines on my cheeks and then smudging my arms and wiping shadows around my eyes. I hand the bowl of what smells like white clay to Skye. Instead of making marks on her face with white and black, Skye sets the bowl aside and just watches us. So this ceremony is just for me—me and Bird.

Is the black and white symbolic of the darkness and light in all of us? Is this supposed to make us see better somehow? I have a dozen questions, but it doesn't seem right to ask them.

Bird closes her eyes, pulls in three deep breaths through her nose that she lets out through her mouth. Opening her eyes, she looks at me and asks, her voice pitched low and soft and her words oddly formal, "Are you ready, Lib of the Tracker Clan?" She doesn't wait for an answer but picks up dried leaves that lay next to the fire circle and tosses them into the flames. The fire licks higher.

Glancing at Skye, I see she sits with her eyes closed and her head tipped back. Her hands rest on her thighs, her palms up and her fingers curved. She almost looks as if she

213

is sleeping. Glancing back to Bird it seems to me that she almost seems older now—different.

Bird waves a hand over the fire, passing her fingers over the flame, making the orange and yellow flickers dance. She glances at me and says, "I will do what I can to help you regain your path—to help you have the vision you need. But you will have to persist on your own after this. Can you follow your path on your own feet by your own will?"

Tension hunches my shoulders. I'm uneasy, but oddly I don't really seem able to move. I can only stare at Bird. The room around me seems soft and the firelight dances over my open palms. Was there something in the clay I put on my skin? I don't know and oddly I don't really care.

"The key to your path is inside you—it is inside us all. But we look away to things and others and even the Outside when we must turn inward instead."

My head seems light as if it will float away from my body. Bird suddenly asks, "When the path demands hardship and sacrifice, are you ready for that?"

Tension slips from my shoulders. My fingertips tingle as do my toes. I should ask what this questions *really* means, but somehow my mouth no longer works. I can only stare at Bird.

She nods as if I had answered and asks, "What do you want most—answers to who you are to become more like the AI?"

It is an odd question to ask, and I puzzle over it, my mind floating now. But I know the answer—I have always known it.

Answers—I want answers.

Answers will give me the means to take down the AI. Answers will tell me who I am. Answers will reveal who Dr. Sig is to me. Answers are everything. That truly is what I search for in the Empties—the answers to everything.

Untying a small, leather drawstring bag from her belt, Bird tugs it open and takes out a pinch of dried leaves. She tosses them into the fire and smoke curls up from the fire, white and weaving into the air like a pale, translucent snake.

I glance over to Skye and see she has opened her eyes. A small smile curves her lips. She looks almost eager to see something happen.

The air smells of spice and of something odd—something that makes me want to rub my nose but I cannot lift my hands. They no longer seem a part of me. I seem to be floating somewhere just outside my body and looking down on the fire, on Skye as she sways and Bird as she starts to chant.

"My clan before was Sees Far Clan from the south and the wasteland. Clan is family. Clan is survival. Clan is all. From the Empties the clans came in the old days, wandering out of destruction to start anew." She pulls out another pinch of dried leaves and throws them onto the fire. More tingling smoke rises up in a column. "Clans learned to survive in the barren wilderness that is the Outside. Clans became more than they were. My clan, my family, learned to see not just to the horizons, but past that point and on to what might be and what will become. Listen now to the beat of your heart. Listen now to the small voice inside. Listen to the gift you carry within you and know that to be human is to accept the responsibility of your gifts."

Bird sounds so serious, I almost want to giggle. I take a deep breath. Smoke fills my nose, making it itch. I release the breath with a whoosh and finally find my word. "Answers."

Bird looks at me. Her eyes seem huge—they are all I see. Eye and the white lines that seem now to point to those dark pools. "This will bring the sight but you have to embrace it."

A warning sounds at the back of my mind, but it seems so distant—as distant as the Empties. I cannot pull it closer. For a heartbeat, I want to stand and leave here. But I cannot move. I cannot even speak now. I can only stare at Bird—at her dark eyes.

Bird gives a nod. "There are two paths in life. One is that of pride. It walls us off from who we are—it has us looking to tools and powers. The other is that of connection to our true selves and to others. It can always lead us home if only we accept it."

None of that makes sense.

Bird waves a hand over the fire, waving the smoke toward me. "Remember always that you are human."

Human. Such an odd word. What does it really mean? I'm a Glitch—a manufactured person. The AI adjusted me somehow—and I need to know how. I need to know why I am connected to the AI—to Conie. Am I just a tool to her? Or am I something more?

The world seems to spin. Glancing over at the painted skin stretched tight on its wooden frame, the old people on it almost seem to move and dance. The trees shiver in a wind and the stars glitter and sparkle.

Bird's voice echoes against the stone. "Humans are born, not made. Look to yourself to find the truth. Look beyond what you wear to see who you are."

Look beyond what I wear—and what do I wear? Skins now—no longer a soft tunic. Skins for boots and pants and a top that has no sleeves. And my biogear. That's what this is about—the biogear? This is a trick—a ploy. A way to try and talk me out of using biogear. I'm so disgusted I want to stand and walk out, but I can't move so much as a finger.

218

Even breathing seems an effort. My heartbeat seems slow and soft.

As if hearing my thoughts, Bird says, "This is about you. And me. And Skye. And all those you touch. You will find the sight within you—you will find what you seek. But your mind has to be open to the truth. How can it be open to who you are if all the time you are giving yourself to an artificial world that has no connection to this one?"

I shiver, cold now. Freezing. My lips numb. Tingles spread over my stomach and slip under my skin.

Bird's voice seems to be inside my head now. *Your path is yours to follow. But you must choose—answers from true vision or your unnatural gear that will forever block you from becoming your true self. You must choose.*

The world darkens. There is only the fire now, dying down, casting dancing shadows against the white walls. The old people on the drawing stop dancing and hide in the shadows. A choice—do I really have one or has Bird taken it from me?

Bird reaches out of the shadows and through the smoke. She touches my forehead with her fingertips, sliding her fingers down my face, trailing over the bridge of my nose and to my lips.

"See with your own eyes," she whispers. "See with your mind. See with your heart. And remember that with each choice there is a consequence."

The smoke swirls up around me—everything seems to be smoke. And one thought keeps sounding the alarm in my mind—what has Bird taken from me?

Chapter Fifteen

I wake back in the women's sleeping room on my own fur, but no one else is with me. How long have I slept? My mouth feels dry and my eyes sting. With a cough, I sit up and my head spins. How long? Getting up, I stumble out and head to the baths. Washing helps clear my head and then I head to the main room—and find the clan eating.

Wolf glances at me, frowning as I stagger into the room. I sit down and lean back against the stone wall, liking how cool it is. Something nudges my arm and I open my eyes— when did I close them? —to find Wolf standing over me and offering a water skin.

"You well?"

I give a grunt and drink some of the water. It's cold and I drink more, and wipe my mouth with the back of my hand. Leaving, Wolf takes the water with him. He comes back with dried fruit. He sits next to me and says, "Eat."

My stomach does a small flip, but I take a sliver of a date—Wolf will just keep pushing food at me. Surprisingly, the fruit tastes good.

"How long?" I ask.

Wolf puts his dark stare on me. "How long what?"

With a shake of my head, I glance around. Skye and Bird aren't here. Light streams in through one of the ceiling holes and there's no fire in the center of the main room, so it must be morning. "Never mind."

Getting to his feet, Wolf keeps staring at me. "Want to see Croc?"

"Do I look that bad?"

"Bad enough you better stay in."

I nod. I feel shaky enough that I don't argue. I eat a little more fruit, drink the water skin dry and then stand and head to the Gear Room. But my stomach clenches when I see the biogear and I almost throw up the food. Staggering away, I head back to the sleeping room and fall down on the fur.

For two days I sleep, getting up only to eat, answer the needs of my body, bathe and sleep again. Whatever Bird did to me seems to have drained my energy. Alis tells me she worries for me, but I ask her to head out with the others and let me know if anything changes at the Norm.

Nothing does—the AI still has scabs working on changing the Norm, and drones guarding the work.

On the third day, I feel better. Stronger. But I've had no visions. No revelations. Nothing. My answers still elude me. And to make matters worse, I can't seem to tolerate the sight of biogear.

Bird has wisely been staying out of my sight—she did something to me. I don't know what was in that smoke, but I fight down nausea every time I look at the biogear. I try to force myself to stay in the Gear Room, but it leaves my head aching and my stomach churning.

At the next evening meal Alis comes over and sits next to me. I have nothing to eat and want nothing and the smell of the meat on Alis's cooking stick has me covering my mouth with a hand.

Alis looks at me and then hands the meat to Dat, who bolts down the food as if someone is going to try and steal it from him.

"What's wrong?" Alis asks. "Not sleeping well?"

I shake my head. What can I say? I let Bird do something to me and now I'm supposed to have visions and answers, but I only feel sick?

Skye comes into the main room. I get up and head over to her. "What did Bird do?"

Stepping back, Skye winces. "Lib, I just know it's hard for you, but it might be easier if you remembered that it was for a good cause."

I feel like rolling my eyes. Instead, I step closer, backing her up against a wall. "What was in that smoke? I get sick even just looking at my biogear. It's killing me."

"No, it's not. It's making you remember to be a person. You don't need that biogear."

Choking down my anger, I can only stare at her. She really thinks that going without the biogear is a good thing —that I'm better. "How do I fight the AI now? You crippled me."

Skye gives a snort, but she looks away and won't meet my eyes. "You fought the AI before without it."

"And almost died."

Skye looks up and puts a hand on my shoulder. "You're important, and you need to see that every person matters. That you are—"

"No." I shake off her hand. "You need to realize we're in a war—and you and Bird might have just condemned us all to death."

*   *   *

Forcing myself to step into the Gear Room I stand there, trembling, and fighting my churning stomach. I gulp down breaths. That seems to help. After five minutes, my stomach settles. My head is pounding, but I can survive that. I force myself to touch my biogear. I manage that much. It's progress. But I can't stand the idea of putting it on.

Alis comes into the room and gives me a sideways glance. "You well?"

"Why does everyone keep asking that?" I demand, annoyed. That also helps fight the queasiness.

Alis lifts a shoulder in a shrug. "Because you don't usually look pale as the moon. You eat some bad meat."

"Something like that."

Sighing, she comes over and stands in front of me. She pushes her curling hair from her face and studies me a moment before saying, "What happened? I can't figure it out. Seems like your suddenly sick at the sight of your own biogear."

Lips pressed tight, fighting the nausea, I nod. "I'll get over it."

She waves her hand at me. "Don't be stupid. You're not well. Something changed. What happened?"

I want to tell her, but what can I say? I let Bird trick me into something? Bird and some odd smoke left me like this? I feel a fool for having trusted Bird. But I also don't want to give up the very faint hope that my answers are still going to come to me. If they do, this will be worth it. Answers can help us more than the biogear—but I fear both are now denied to me.

Turning from Alis, I give a halfhearted shrug. "It's just...I'm not feeling well. All this...this craziness...I think it caught up to me. I just need...need to get some rest. We've been pushing too hard."

Alis heads back to her own gear, and my stomach does a flip. "That's because we have to. You said the AI isn't going to wait for us to figure out what it's doing."

*   *   *

I have no choice but to hope Bird really was trying to give me visions and answers—and wasn't just tricking me into not being able to use biogear. I can't really explain this to Alis, so I head to the sleeping room. Just being around the biogear has left me drained.

Lying on my fur leaves me restless and turning. I'm angry with myself for trusting Skye, for letting Bird lead me into a trap. I was stupid. But was I really?

But what if Bird's smoke is a lot like biogear—what if it doesn't work for some people? What if it's dependent on each person's biology? What if I really am to different— and not quite human.

That leaves me shuddering and pulling another fur over me even though it is warm in the sleeping room.

I can't sleep—I am not having visions. Or even dreams. Getting up, I head to the main room, stepping over the sleeping forms of others who have come in to rest.

What will I do if I can't use biogear? How can I go anywhere? What use am I? I can't even work on any biogear right now.

The knowledge makes me want so hit something, so I head to the Gear Room, grab a lamp, fight down the churning in my stomach and head to the training room.

No one is training at his hour—the clan is either asleep, on watch, or out on a scavenge. I am the one stuck here. Staring at the empty space of the training room, the oil lamp warm in my hand and casting a yellow glow around me, I wonder now if Bird wasn't right in a way. Have I become my biogear?

Without it I'm not so confident in my abilities. I'm slower. I'm not very strong.

I'm back to feeling like the misplaced Glitch I was when I was first tossed out of the Norm.

A soft step behind me makes me turn. Wolf steps out of the shadows, his broad shoulders filling up the tunnel behind him. He has a way of making the training room seem small. But he looks…tired. A smear of purple smudges appear beneath his dark eyes and his shoulders slump in a way I've never seen before. I don't like it.

"Not sleeping?" he asks. He sounds weary.

I hesitate and shrug. "You're not out on a scavenge?"

A frown tugs at his full lips. "Didn't send anyone out. Like you said, connects are getting harder. No hacks means no water. You training?"

Suddenly, I wish I could. But I'm tired again—as tired as Wolf looks. I head over to one of the rocks that makes for a seat. Wolf trails after me, but he doesn't sit down. Irritation pricks at me. "What's wrong with us?"

Wolf shakes his head. "Us…or you? You think I haven't seen. Not eating. No gear. You're vulnerable without your gear."

"Maybe I want to learn how to live without it. I thought you didn't like the biogear anyway."

He purses his lips together and for a moment says nothing. He runs a hand through his hair and says, "Doesn't mean I don't know we need it. AI's making it harder to get water—harder for anything. AI's getting ready to do something."

Looking up at him, I wonder if he knows I have Otter, Crow, Alis, Pike, Hawk and Star keeping an eye on the Norm. But how would Wolf know. Shadows hide his eyes from me. I can't see his expression. Instead of asking about what he said, I ask, "Why didn't you send out a scavenge? We'll be running low on water in just a few days."

He lifts a hand and lets it fall. "Why send out if you can't bring anything back. The old platforms are dry. We can't get to the ones by the Norm."

Frowning, I dig the toe of my boot into the sand. The oil lamp is getting too warm in my hand so I set it down on the rock next to me. Then I look up at Wolf. "Why tell me this?"

He hesitates and then says, "Because I care about you, Lib. Trouble's brewing in the clan. Don't know that I can stop it. Don't know that I should. Food we can hunt, but clan won't survive without water. May mean we need to move again soon. May mean change is coming. May mean your biogear really is what will save us."

Before I can process his words, he leans down, sweeping in with a fast move. His mouth fits over mine. My eyes flutter closed. His lips are warm and the taste of him sweeter than anything I've known.

His arms go around my waist and he pulls me up and holds me close against him. I can feel his heart beating fast —mine's even faster. All I want suddenly is to stay here with him. To let him kiss me as long as he wants.

But he lets me go as fast as he swept me up, leaving me unsteady on my feet. He disappears down the tunnels. I touch a hand to my lips. What did he mean trouble's coming—and why is he changing his mind about biogear now that I can't use it?

Chapter Sixteen

It takes me two more days to force myself into my biogear. I do it on an empty stomach, gulping down air, alone in the Gear Room.

Only to find it no longer works for me.

If Bird was anywhere near me, I would stick Raj's knife into her—but I can't do that. Clan law says disputes can be solved with a challenge, but never with a death. That's waste—that means instant banishment. I have to settle for stripping off my biogear and trying to adapt it to work with me now.

The only bright moment I have to hold onto is Wolf's kiss.

The memory of it leaves a warmth spreading through my chest, but I keep worrying what Wolf meant about trouble coming. The news that the AI is shutting down old platforms also worries me—it sounds as if she really is getting ready, or maybe the water is running out. Either is very bad news.

Struggling with my biogear, I strip out components and find nothing works for me—but the power is working. I have to figure out how to adapt it to whatever that smoke did to me. Or hope the smoke wears off.

Or I have to learn how to fight the AI with only Raj's knife. That seems a very good way to die.

Alis comes into the Gear Room along with Star and a report on the Norm. Star has short, black hair and skin that is almost black. She and Alis seem almost opposites, but they also seem to be building a friendship.

I often wonder how they do that. Friendship does not come easy to me and I wonder if it's because all I can think about is defeating the AI and saving Raj. I seem to have only known struggle and nothing else. Or maybe it is because I have so few memories. Maybe that's why it is easier to be with Wolf—he doesn't like talking very much, so being with him is just a matter of being.

"Where are the others?" I ask Alis.

She glances at Star and says, "Who knows? Crow's been in a mood lately. I don't know who ground a stone into his heart, but he's been worse than you."

I let that remark go past and ask, "Have you heard anything about trouble in the clan?""

Star and Alis share another glance and Star says, "We're on water rations. Haven't had a scavenge go right now in four times out."

That is why Wolf worries. "That's not good. We're going to have to see if we can do a connect closer to the Norm."

Alis opens her mouth to say something, but Crow and Hawk walk into the Gear Room. It's getting crowded.

Hawk is complaining about something. Crow turns on him. "Enough. You talk more than anyone I've ever met."

Hawk snaps his mouth shut. He steps away from Crow and with a hunched shoulder leans against the far wall. "Someone say something about a connect?"

Heading to the opposite wall, Crow says, "What good is that? Water's drying up. Bound to happen sometime. AI's sucked everything dry."

"We don't know that." I glance around. Everyone seems wound tight as a coiled wire. I've been so caught up in my own misery I have missed the tension within the clan—I'm seeing it now. This is not good—if the clan falls apart there is no one to fight the AI.

Is this her plan?

"We need to change priorities—get some water in," I tell them.

Crow makes a derisive noise in his throat. "If we can," he mutters.

I shoot him a look. He stares back at me, so I tell him, "This doesn't mean our goals change. We still need to know what's going on with the AI. But it's hard to do that if we don't have enough water to live on."

Straightening, Crow says, "Let Wolf worry about the water. He's clan leader, isn't he?"

I'm surprised by Crow's vehemence. Taking a deep breath, I try to stay reasonable even though irritation is picking at me and my stomach is knotting again. "He is, and clan still looks after clan. All of this is supposed to be about saving lives."

Star shakes her head and says, "You'll come with us? Make the connect and hack the system for water?"

My stomach does a flip and twists tighter. I swallow, bite my lower lip, but I nod. I don't want to go out without biogear—I don't want to put it on. I'm going to have to figure out how to make this work.

For a second, everyone's quiet. I'm waiting for another angry outburst from Crow, but he lets out a sigh and shakes his head. "We can handle this with Alis. Lib hasn't been feeling well lately."

I'm surprised he noticed and I can only stare at him. "No. I'll...I can go." My words sound weak to me. "I want to go."

Crow's features soften ever so slightly. The scar down his cheek leaves his mouth slightly twisted up on one side. He fixes me with an intense stare that seems full of meaning, but I'm not sure what that meaning is. "You don't have to do this, Lib. We can handle a scavenge. You think this is important. Let us do this for you."

I don't want to say yes. I need to get back into my biogear. But the clan needs water—it's a more immediate need than stopping the AI because we can't live without it. But I worry—can Alis make a connect on her own? Can she hack the system and find the water?

Glancing at my biogear, I reach out and touch it. My stomach clenches and I have to put a hand on my side. But I don't throw up. That's got to be progress.

With a heavy sigh, I turn to Crow. "Okay. But be careful. And we'll all see about heading back to the Norm tomorrow to see what progress the AI is making."

*   *   *

Crow's anger leaves me worried. He is wearing his biogear all the time now, and I don't know if it is changing him.

Is this what Bird saw in me—changes? But others are also irritable—even Dat and Alis get into an argument and Dat never fights with anyone.

Water rations are partly to blame. We are down to only one water storage cistern full, and Alis comes back with the others with only two containers of water. She shakes her head at me and tells me the hack barely worked.

Wolf takes out a scavenge to get water from plants, but the rains are late this year. I could almost wish for the kind of rain I saw on the moving images, with water pouring down in a flood. I can't decide which is worse—no water or too much.

Heading to the main room for the evening meal, I at least know I can take my biogear apart. I also can make the screen work, so maybe whatever Bird did to me is wearing off. Bird is no longer avoiding me, but I don't want to talk to her—I will end up hitting her if I do

I'm almost to the main room when I hear raised voices. I frown and quicken my pace. Stepping into the main room I glance around. A group of five is gathered around Crow and Badger, one of the older clan members.

"All you do is complain," Badger says, spitting the words at Crow. He pushes Crow in the chest.

"And you don't even do that," Crow shouts, his hand balling into a fist.

Panic sizzles through me. Crow is going to hit Beaver, and if this escalates, Crow could end up in real trouble. I hurry forward and catch Crow's arm. "Stop it." Glancing at Badger, I include him in the order.

Crow lets out a breath, but Badger shakes his head. "Let him. Then he'll see what clan law really is."

I glance around at the other Rogues—I can see disgust in their eyes. Are they disappointed I stopped a fight? I wave them away, asking if they have nothing better to do and turn to Crow. "What was that all about?"

"What else? Wolf—and everything he's not doing."

Instantly, I'm furious. "Crow, the problems we're facing are a result of what the AI is doing—not because of Wolf!"

Crow glances at me, his face hard. "I'm not the only one who thinks Wolf has lost his path."

He turns and walks away from me.

His path.

I am left thinking of what Bird told me—that she would help me find my path. That I had to do that without biogear.

Is the biogear pulling others away from their paths? Is it creating problems within the clan? Even if it is, how can we possibly fight the AI without it?

I need to get back into my biogear if I even have a hope of getting into the Norm again—and suddenly it no longer matters to me if I have to give up my answers.

I have to help the clan.

Chapter Seventeen

I spend two more days fighting to get myself into my biogear and get it working. It does—in fits and starts. It's unreliable now. I also have to break up a fight between Star and Hawk and another between Dat and Dog, who I found rolling around in the tunnels, trying to punch each other.

And the water in the cistern keeps going lower.

Tensions seem higher now. Wolf does what he can, but everyone is thirsty and unhappy. Three scavenges go out and only one brings back one container of water.

Wolf is right—the AI is shutting down the platforms, closing off all water. I worry this means she is getting closer to leaving, and I still have no idea how to stop her or slow her down.

The fractures within the clan have Bird avoiding anyone with biogear. And even the council argues—I hear them one day when I am walking down the tunnels. It is clear they can agree on nothing.

I spot Wolf striding down the tunnel, and I am surprised he is not in with the council. As he passes me, he reaches out and trails a finger over the back of my hand and then he heads away from me, frowning and obviously trying to figure out something to get the clan water.

I wish I had an idea.

I head to the baths—we have water there, but it is impossible to drink it. Too much sulfur and other minerals that can kill you. We can wash with it, but that's it.

Alis is there, sitting near the water, scanning it with her biogear screen. She looks up and shuts off the screen. "Dat thought maybe we could figure out a way to pull the minerals out of the water so we could drink it."

I sit down next to her. "Good idea. Can we?"

Alis shakes her head. "I don't know how. Lib, are we… is the clan going to split apart?"

Sitting down next to her, I take off my boots and roll up my pants and stick my feet in the warm water. "I don't know. I keep trying to know more—to get answers and it all just falls apart on me. It's like I'm not meant to know some things."

Alis nods. "There are times I feel like that—just frustrated. And then I get outside in the biogear and it all just slips away and it's just me moving as fast as I can. I feel like I can outrun the world then."

I bite my lip. Envy chokes me. I want that feeling again. But do I really? Looking sideways at Alis, I ask, "Do you think the biogear changed you?"

She frowns. "How do I know? You're on the outside. Do you think it changed me?" she asks.

"Yes…and no. You've gotten better working with the gear. That's not bad. You're stronger. You go out and make connects on your own. Maybe…maybe the truth is complicated. Maybe…maybe we have to change. But we also should be working together. That's how we're going to survive." I kick my feet in the pool, appreciating the warmth of the water.

Alis activates her biogear screen and stares at the water. "We think groups are more powerful than the individual, but doesn't the AI show us the opposite is true? The AI is one thing that is more powerful than anything else."

"She is not!" I snap out the words, but my face heats and I know I'm reacting to my fear that this is really true. Taking a deep breath, I glance at Alis. "Sorry. I just don't think we should make the AI out to be more than she is. She is a system—a big one and very smart. But she is not a person. I will never allow that she is some great thing."

Alis switches off her biogear. "Okay, then what about Wolf? Is he some great thing? And if he is, why doesn't he come up with a way to fight the AI? Or a way to at least get us water?"

I let out a huff of air. "That is something for everyone to do. A leader isn't the person who should tell you what to do. I mean, think about Bird. This is her failing. She wants others to do as she wants—she pushes. She pushed me into giving up biogear."

Alis stares at me. "She did? How?"

I shake my head. "That is a long story—but you need to see the point here. Wolf doesn't push. He pulls at us. I'm not sure the Tracker Clan would even be here without him."

Alis shakes her head and stands. "If Wolf was really a leader, he'd be wearing biogear and he'd be leading us into battle with the AI. And it'd be a battle we could win. Don't let your feelings for him blind you, Lib. Wolf is really just another Rogue who is stuck in how things have always been. Sometimes I think we'd all be better off just going up against the AI and dying in a blaze of battle. That'd be an end to it."

*   *   *

My conversation with Alis leaves me thinking about Wolf and if I really am letting my feelings blind me. Is she right? Do I owe him so much because he did save me— more than once?

I'm frustrated that I don't have my answers as Bird said I would. I have no path. Whatever she did left me crippled, not made whole. Fighting down the headache and nausea, I put on my biogear and manage to get the communication blocking noise to work, but I end up throwing up my food. I strip off the biogear and rip it apart, hating it, hating what Bird did to me, hating myself for being a fool enough to let her. When my biogear is in pieces, I walk out, heading to the main room.

As usual, tension hangs in the room. Everyone is down to just two cups of water a day and it's leaving everyone angry and ready to snap.

Wolf steps between Dog and Badger, breaking up an argument. He moves away and we lock stares for the briefest of seconds before voices start to rise again.

"If they're going to wear gear, they should do it outside." Komodo mutters the words. I glance over and see him sitting with Bird and Gazelle.

My stomach tightens, but for once it's not from the biogear. Glancing around, I see Dat, Crow, Otter and Pike have worn their gear to the meal. They seem to be wearing their gear all the time—maybe it is addictive.

I start to walk over to Wolf who is standing in front of Komodo now.

"Gear," Komodo spits out the word. "Makes them something that's not even human!"

Pike moves faster than Komodo can. She's on him in a flash, her fist making solid contact with his face. Komodo stands, but Wolf holds him back. I head to grab Pike before she can hit Komodo again. A trickle of blood drips from his nose.

Holding Komodo back, Wolf mutters, "Enough. We are not the enemy. Save the fight for something that needs killing"

"What do you know anyway?" Pike jerks away from my hold.

My biogear usually makes me stronger. Without it, I can't match Pike's strength. I step between her and Komodo and Wolf. "Pike, don't waste energy. You know the law—waste nothing."

For a moment, I think she's going to ignore me and go after Komodo again. But she shoots me a hard look and says, "I was defending you." Turning, she strides away and disappears down one of the tunnels.

Komodo pulls away from Wolf and locks stares with him. "You're losing control of the clan."

Wolf shakes his head. "There is no law that everyone must keep their tempers at all times. Clan has no law of control over all—and I'm not Lib's AI."

Shock rushes through me, leaving me light headed. *Lib's AI?* Is that what Wolf thinks? As if I invented the AI? Or as if I am a part of her. I stagger back a step.

Silence fills the room. Only the crackle of the fire can be heard. I realize everyone's watching us. I glance at Wolf and see the regret in his eyes.

He knows what he just said. Lib's AI. As if I made up everything I said about her wanting to leave this world and take the Norm with her—he doesn't really believe that is possible.

Turning away, I stumble from the room. Behind me, I hear Wolf telling the others we must work together, how we are clan.

I don't want to hear any of it.

I see now why Bird hates the biogear—she fears it links me to the AI. I see why Wolf fears the biogear—for he, too, sees it linking me to the AI.

And for once I see my path—I am linked to the AI. I cannot escape that. Bird was wrong about my path being one separate from the biogear. I can never escape the AI. Conie's fate and mine are linked.

Behind me, I hear soft steps and turn to see Wolf following me. He comes up to me and I lean my back against the tunnel wall. I'll fall if I don't. "These fights are getting worse," he tells me, his voice soft and worry leaking into his words.

I only nod.

He stands in front of me and puts his hands on my shoulders. "I want you to know, I don't care about the talk. I care about you. You are someone special to me, Lib."

His words catch me off guard and I don't know what to say. But the hurt from his words eats at me. "I care about you, too. But…Lib's AI. She's not mine. I don't control her. But I am going to find a way to end her. You just keep your clan together so they're there when the battle comes." Pulling away from him, I stagger off to the Gear Room to try and make my biogear work again.

Chapter Eighteen

Wolf keeps the fighting under control...until Komodo issues a challenge.

I hear about it from Hawk who comes to the Gear Room the next day to say I have to come to the training room.

"Lib, you've got to come. Komodo's just told Wolf he's not fit to lead. They're going to fight over it and if Komodo wins...." He trails off. But he doesn't have to say the rest. There are only a few ways to become clan leader. A leader can be chosen by the council—or can be challenged to a fight and the winner becomes the new leader. If that happens...Komodo's made it clear he won't tolerate any biogear. He'll probably even banish me—and push the council into approving it.

I stare at Hawk, and he asks me, "Don't you want to see this?"

"You go ahead. I'll catch up."

He shrugs, turns and hurries away.

I have to take several deep breaths to calm the shaking inside.

Komodo as clan leader—it will be disaster. Everything we've worked for will be lost. Wolf may not really believe the AI can leave this world, but Komodo doesn't think we should even be fighting the AI. I knew that when I heard him speak in council about how I was the one stirring up trouble with the AI.

Hurrying, I head to the training room. It is already crowded and it seems as if everyone in the clan is here. Light filters down from the holds in the ceiling, spilling onto a circle drawn into the sand. That is the fight area.

Wolf stands by himself, his shirt off, his head down and his arms crossed, and he looks as if he is about to fall asleep, his eyes are half closed. I move closer to him, nudging my way past others. Komodo isn't a small man and neither is Wolf. Judging by the grim expression on Komodo's face—his set mouth, the sharp light in his eyes —this is going to be an ugly fight.

Before I reach Wolf, Bird catches my arm and says, "Don't."

251

I haven't spoken to her since she took away my ability to use biogear. Now I stare at her and pull away from her. "Stay out of my way."

Shaking her head, she moves in front of me. "You don't understand. This is a challenge. Wolf has to fight or step down as leader. And you have no right to interfere."

I push Bird out of my way. "Haven't you done enough damage already?" Brushing past her, I head to Wolf's side and stop in front of him. "Do you know what you're doing?"

His eyes open a little wider. He glances around the crowded training room and then looks back at me. "You don't have to watch. But this is necessary."

I glance over at Komodo. He's taken off his shirt. He is thicker than Wolf in the middle, meaning he carries more muscle. But Wolf has the longer reach. Turning back to Wolf, I ask, "Can you beat him?"

Wolf just lifts his chin and stares at me, so I ask, "Can you beat him if you wear biogear? There's no law about that."

He shakes his head. "There is no law. But this isn't just a test of strength. Cunning matters as well. I must prove I can lead."

I nod and glance again at Komodo. He bares his teeth at me in an unpleasant smile.

Turning back to Wolf, I stare up at him. His eyes are dark, intense as ever and just a little sad. I give a nod. "Then win. Win because if you don't, Komodo won't try to fight the AI. Win because if you don't, Komodo will try to control the clan. Win because if you don't, Komodo will throw me from the clan and you won't be able to do anything about it. Win—or we all die."

Wolf's head comes up. My words seem to sink into him and he gives a small nod. I don't know if he is agreeing with my assessment, but I am hoping it spurs him on to win at any cost.

His mouth lifts a little and he says, "Now you speak like a true Rogue."

Komodo calls out his challenge again, so everyone here can hear it. "I, Komodo of Tracker Clan, call Wolf to account. I say Wolf is no longer fit to lead Tracker Clan. I challenge Wolf as leader."

Reaching out, I give Wolf's hand a squeeze. I slip into the crowd. I find Alis and stand next to her. She doesn't have her biogear on and seems almost uninterested in all of this. "You don't agree with this challenge as a method of choosing leaders?" I guess.

She glances at me. "Seems a good way to end up with a bully and a gorilla for a leader."

"Wolf says it's about cunning, too."

"He better be right," Alis says over the shouts of the clan that rise up around us. "Because Komodo looks ready to kill."

Glancing over at the two, now facing each other, I think she is right. Wolf and Komodo step into the crudely drawn circle. Wolf offers his hand to Komodo. Komodo shakes his head and slaps the gesture away.

From the crowd, I hear Crow give a shout. And Komodo strikes first with a kick aimed at Wolf's side and belly.

He's fast and he obviously doesn't care if he hurts Wolf, perhaps with a fatal blow. Wolf dodges, and Komodo's kick skims along Wolf's side. I expect Wolf to hit back, but he simply moves carefully around the circle, his eyes locked on his opponent.

It looks like Komodo says something to him, but everyone else seems to be shouting, calling out moves or encouragement to Wolf or Komodo.

Komodo lunges at Wolf, aiming a blow with his fist to Wolf's head. Again, Wolf ducks. The hit lands on Wolf's shoulder. Komodo staggers and falls forward slightly.

Wolf seems to simply step in and he catches Komodo's neck in the crook of his arm. Wolf steps again, coming up around behind Komodo. Sweat glistens on Komodo's bald scalp and his eyes widen. He reaches up to grab Wolf's arm. Wolf tightens his hold, and Komodo, his face red, tugs at Wolf's arm desperately.

For a moment they struggle, both men gasping, then Komodo jabs an elbow into Wolf's ribs. Wolf gasps and Komodo slips out of Wolf's grip. Turning, Komodo rubs at his throat and then charges Wolf. Komodo starts to hit out with his left hand, but shifts suddenly and swings his right arm, landing a fist against Wolf's face. The hard slap of flesh against flesh makes me flinch. Wolf staggers back, blood dripping from his nose. Komodo swings again, a sloppy blow that Wolf blocks with his forearm.

They close on each other, exchanging blows that set more blood flying and carry the hard crack of knuckles and bones breaking. Wolf steps back, almost to the edge of the circle. Komodo follows him, his head down, kicking and punching. Wolf's bleeding, but his eyes look calm to me. I can see Komodo's side heaving as he struggles for breath. Sweat glistens on his skin. Red streaks his face and on his hands. Wolf takes a hard kick to the stomach and seems to fall from the force of it, but I notice that Wolf turns and lands flat on his back as if he wants Komodo to follow him to the ground.

Komodo seems to act without thought, falling on Wolf. Dust swirls into the room, torn from the sand on the ground. I cough and wave away the fine grains. Others shout. For a moment, I fear Komodo has his hands around Wolf's throat.

Wolf is on his back with Komodo on top of him. Wolf's mouth quirks. He wraps his legs around Komodo's ribs, shifts and suddenly Komodo is thrown from the fighting circle. Komodo's body flies, the crowd parts and Komodo slams into the rock wall. He gives a groan and lays still. Wolf stands and walks over to Komodo. He puts a foot on Komodo's throat. The room suddenly falls silent.

"Do you still challenge?" Wolf asks.

Komodo gives a gurgle and shakes his head. Blood drips into his eyes. His sides are still heaving and he holds a hand against his ribs. Wolf takes his foot off Komodo's throat. He offers his hand to Komodo to help him up. Reluctantly, mouth twisted down, Komodo pushes up to his knees. He staggers to his feet and only then does he take Wolf's hand.

*   *   *

Croc insists on patching up both men, and tells them the whole time that he has seen small boys offer up a better display of skill and cunning and they both should be ashamed of their prowess.

I listen to all of it and keep asking Wolf if he broke anything. Wolf just smiles.

Komodo refuses to stay in Croc's room. Croc gives him ointment for his ribs and tells him to soak in the baths. Komodo shoots me a stare and stalks away as if he doesn't want to listen to anyone.

I sit beside Wolf as Croc puts ointment on the smaller cuts and tells Wolf he broke a finger and his bruises will bloom like cactus after a rain.

"Put this on them," Croc says and hands Wolf the leaf off a plant. "And drink this if you have too much pain to sleep."

Wolf waves away the small skin of whatever would make him sleep. "Save that for someone in need."

I shake my head, and Croc throws up his hands. "Then I've done all I can for you. I can't cure stubborn. Rest and heal." He glances at me. "Meaning don't worry him for a day. I'm going to go eat."

Croc leaves, muttering about youth and stupidity like he's ancient. Which he's not.

When he's gone, I turn to Wolf. "I'm glad you won."

He nods, touches his side where Komodo kicked him and which is turning purple, and winces. "There was no doubt of it." Reaching out, he catches my hand. "Lib—I did not mean to say the AI is yours alone. We are tied to our enemies—they make us who we are."

My throat tightens. I still do not like this idea, but I lean forward and press a gentle kiss to his cheek—the one that isn't bruised. "I'll bring you food."

Water is still under ration, but Crow and Otter brought back fresh meat today, so there is plenty to eat. The mood in the main room seems almost festive—a good change from how things have been. I pick up two sticks of roast meat and head back to see if Wolf is hungry—but I almost expect him to be asleep.

I expect Croc to be there and fussing, but I hear Wolf laugh and that shocks me.

Then I hear Bird's voice.

Looking into Croc's healing room, I see Bird sitting next to Wolf, her ribbons fluttering as she describes how the fight would have gone if she'd challenged Wolf. She is punching his arm lightly. She looks tiny next to him. Delicate. Wolf smiles again and wraps a hand around Bird's small fist.

In that moment I see they share more than I ever knew.

Hurt and jealousy both race through me until I feel like I'm going to choke. I look at the food in my hands and suddenly feel stupid. Bird and Wolf have a bond I will never know. They are alike in the way I am so very unlike everyone else. I am intruding where I do not belong.

Looking down and away, I turn and leave.

I take the food to Dat, who eats anything he is given, and then I head to the Gear Room.

Wolf is right. I am tied to the AI—to my enemy. I will never have a life until she is gone. But now, doing away with her no longer seems frightening—if I die and she dies as well that will be a good trade.

Chapter Nineteen

Working on the biogear still leaves me ill, but I almost have it working. It is no longer biogear—it is now tools I have to strap on and carry. I can make the screen work or the communication blocking noise. I cannot activate the extra strength—every time I try to connect the biogear to me it starts a connect and pulls out. This leaves me worried that I won't ever be able to make a connect—meaning I won't be able to hack into the Norm.

Alis reports back that the work on the Norm seems to be slowing—this worries me. We may be out of time.

Wolf comes to the Gear Room—it is the first time he has been here. For a moment he won't step inside, but then he takes a breath and walks in. I wonder then if Bird gave him the same thing she gave me—something that makes his stomach churn at even the sight of biogear. I want to ask him about that, but I worry that it will leave me sounding like I am complaining about Bird. Instead I ask, "How's Komodo?"

Wolf waves a hand. "Komodo is Komodo. He was born angry."

"So…not something he's going to get over."

"No. But he won't challenge me again for a few months at least."

I stare at him. "He's done that before?"

Wolf nods and shrugs. He comes over and stares at my biogear parts. "Didn't this used to be something you put on?"

"I've been changing things. I can still wear it." And I hope those words get back to Bird. I don't want her to know her trick worked in even a small way. It's petty of me, but it was even more petty of her to be so underhanded.

Straightening, Wolf fixes that deep, intense stare of his on me. "Are you angry?"

I have to catch my breath. It's too easy to forget how direct he can be. "Not…angry."

"Disappointed? You disapprove of the challenge? That I had to fight. I thought you were bringing me food."

Sucking in a breath, I look up at him. "You were busy with Bird. I don't get along with Bird anymore."

His expression goes blank. It really looks like he has no idea what I'm talking about. I can practically see his mind searching for answers. "I know. The biogear—she hates it. It's come...between you."

"That's not all between us," I mutter.

Wolf glances around. There is nowhere to sit. He takes my hand, sits on the floor and pulls me down to sit next to him. I try to resist, but it's like resisting a strong wind. Still holding my hand, he tells me, "When Bird first came to the Tracker Clan, many thought her a good choice for leader or leader's mate. I wasn't leader, but clans do ally like that."

Frowning, I ask, "So you became clan leader and now you're supposed to take Bird to stand with you?"

He pats my hand. "It was an idea. I wasn't opposed. But Bird and I became friends—nothing more. And then Raj came."

"Raj? What does he have to do with this?"

"Bird felt a connection. I don't understand all Bird knows or sees…or why she likes people. Or doesn't like. Or why she changes. But Bird looked at Raj as she looked at no one else."

The mention of Raj sends a wash of pain through me. Now I wonder how much worse it is for Bird to have lost him.

"I don't know if Raj felt the same. Bird never said. But she feels his loss."

His mouth twists up on one side and down on the other. "And Skye found you and things changed."

He holds my gaze. My chest tightens. "But I think that may be why there are so many problems now. I wish I hadn't come. The AI sent me out to find the Glitches—she wanted to destroy the Glitches and Rogues so you wouldn't take resources. But…my failure pushed her into planning to leave." My voice is barely a whisper.

His eyebrows pull together. "No. I cannot believe that. Look at what the AI does—taking all the resources, not trying to make the world better. The AI's plans to leave have been long in the making. And you did not listen when I spoke to the others. We are clan. We must work together."

"I want to think you're right about the AI—about her plans. But if you're serious about working with each other, we have to talk about something else." I put my hand over his. "I have to go back into the Norm."

Chapter Twenty

"He sits up a little, tension stiffening his shoulders.

Just get it out. "You have to know those wearing biogear have been watching the Norm."

Something glitters in his dark eyes. I'm not sure if it's anger or amusement. "Watching is not a bad thing. But it sounds as if you have other plans, too."

"I knew you weren't going to like this. But…well, if Bird has feelings for Raj, that makes it more important. I need to find Raj. He may not be dead—and if he's alive, he might know how to stop the AI. That's why he went back —to find out how to change the AI.

Shaking his head, he mutters something I don't catch. In a louder voice, he says, "When did you plan to tell me? Or did you want to do this all without help?"

"I do not even know how to get back into the Norm. I just know we're running out of time. The AI has been making changes to the Norm and seems to be finishing them. And how could I tell you any of this without you starting to do this?"

"This?"

"You had other problems—including water, which is still a problem. And I seem to remember saying something in council about needing to do something about the AI."

He leans his head back against the wall. He still holds my hand. "Yes. But what I heard was an argument about your biogear. I did not listen well that day."

I'm not sure what to say now. I trace a purple line—a vein—on the back of his hand.

Lifting his head, Wolf looks at me and asks, "Tell me all you have found out?"

Talking about the Norm and what we've learned makes me realize how little information we have. I don't even know what the AI is changing. Is she making the dome stronger? Changing the power? I hate being outside and not knowing.

Wolf listens, a small frown drawing a line between his eyebrows. After a moment, he says, "You were wise not to go too close and alert the AI. You talk of scabs—"

"It's a name I remember from…from when I think I was a Tech inside the Norm."

He taps my forehead with a finger. "Ah, you do have memories. Do you think these scabs have weapons?"

"No. If they did, they wouldn't need drones to be guarding the work. The AI seems to see everything as having one function—everything except her. The scabs seemed focused entirely on building."

He nods. "It seems we know everything possible to know from outside. I see why you talk of going back into the Norm. The question is how?" He squeezes my hand, lets go and stands. I scramble to my feet as well. Wolf glances at the biogear. "Do you really think this will help you?"

I have to shake my head. "Yes and no. At one time—it really was the answer. Or it was the only answer I could see. I've proven the biogear doesn't pull in drones, but… well, it does do something to the wearer. Bird wasn't wrong about that. The cost seems worth it, given what we're up against. But…maybe Bird had a point, too, about needing to look after each of us—that we all matter. I'm still not convinced about that. We're up against an AI that wants to destroy the world. It seems like one person doesn't matter so much compared with that."

Wolf paces across the room and back again. "Everyone does matter. We cannot give up that idea. But we are out of time—because we are almost out of water. I hoped we had more time—time to become stronger, to learn more, to… well, to live. But that hope is dead. It seems we must act— we must find a way to get into the Norm. But you are not gong alone. And you are not going with just one person. We need the help of clan. It is time for you to learn what many can do."

Chapter Twenty-One

I've been to council meetings and to the ceremony where the clan remembers those gone from us—those who die. I have never seen the clan gather for all to listen and speak. Even Komodo is here, still looking a little yellow from his bruises.

I ask Alis and the others to leave off the biogear. I am starting to think the biogear increases whatever is needed to run fast and be strong—and those same things inside the body also make someone more aggressive. A long time in biogear means a lot of aggression coming out. Crow isn't happy about leaving off his biogear, but no one else seems to mind.

Wolf glances around the room and raises his hands. Talk stops and Wolf begins to tell a story.

For a moment I think that Wolf's story is irrelevant, but I start to realize he is telling the story of the Norm—how a dome was put over the people to keep them safe. How it became a prison. How it now threatens us all. It is everything I know about the AI and the Norm and it is odd to hear it come from Wolf's mouth.

Looking around the room, I see Skye leaning her chin on her hand and listening to Wolf talk. She already knows most of this story—as a Glitch, a former Tech, she has been inside the Norm.

When Wolf finishes talking, he turns to Skye and calls out to her. "Skye, you come to clan from the Norm. You were a Tech. Tell us what you know of the AI who rules the Norm."

Skye stands. She wets her lips, glances around and tugs on the tips of her hair. She clears her throat and starts to talk. "You know me as Skye who was once a Glitch. The AI discards what is needed. The AI does not know the law that nothing is wasted, for the AI will waste people and gear. But the AI does good, too. The AI runs the Norm and makes it function."

"We should destroy that thing," Gazelle calls out.

But Komodo lifts his head. "No, we should leave the AI alone so it leaves us to our own lives."

Wolf lifts his hands again. "Skye talks now. Others will have a turn."

Skye swallows and tugs on her hair again. "I know that a lot of the clan feels as Gazelle does. I understand why. The AI has caused a lot of problems for a lot of people— but I think we're missing all the good the AI has done, too. The AI is just a machine."

Bird gives a harsh laugh. "And a machine can never be bad? They destroy things and ruin this world."

Skye shakes her head and frowns. "That's not true. This world was damaged and the AI saved people by taking them under the control of the Norm. That's how people survived. If the AI hadn't done that, maybe none of us would be here now."

Dog calls out, "How do you know this?"

Mouth opening and closing, Skye shakes her head. "I… it's just what everyone in the Norm knows."

"Because the AI told you," Otter says, his voice low.

A shiver runs down my back. I wish I could get Otter into the same room as the AI—I doubt even she could survive his hatred.

Skye takes a deep breath. "The Norm is a nice place to live. With green grass and tall trees and food and games."

"And water," Dat mutters and licks his lips.

"And the AI put you outside for having seizures," I call out. "And the AI turned the Techs into mindless monsters ready to kill me and Raj."

Skye sits down, her face pale. She bows her head and stares at her hand.

"Lib, you would talk?" Wolf calls out.

It's my turn to have to lick my lips and stand. I glance around the room and find some eyes seem interested, others look hostile, and Crow seems bored as if he already has all his answers. "The Norm could be a much easier place to live." I glance at Komodo and use the words he once threw at me in council. "But as someone once told me, easier does not mean *better*. The AI offers a trade— live for her, to maintain her, and you can live. But is it life

273

to have no choice but to obey, for the AI gives no choice." Bird is nodding agreement with me, her eyes cold and her face tense. It's almost chilling how much she hates the AI.

"You all know my story. You know how I came here and how I returned to the Norm and came out again. You know the story I told of the AI wishing to leave this world, but I am done telling you what to do. That's what the AI does—that's what Conie does. Maybe you can find a place to live far from here with water. I don't think so. But, then, I have my opinions and they aren't for the here and now. I know the AI has to be stopped. It is too far gone, too corrupted. But I also know I want answers. I want to know who my family is. I want to know why the AI is so determined to destroy us." I glance at Bird again. "And I want to know where Raj is, because I have to believe he's alive. These are all things only the AI can answer for me. But I may have to choose between answers—and all of our lives. If that choice comes…I've made wrong choices in the past. This time I want to make a better one."

Bird stands and asks, "And do you choose to use biogear?"

Chapter Twenty-Two

After I speak, the meeting seems to become arguments. Bird's words seem to widen the rift between those who use biogear and those who don't trust it. Crow walks out. Alis argues for the biogear. Otter says nothing but sits and scowls at everyone who speaks against the biogear. Komodo again talks of relocating the clan, but I notice he stops talking when Wolf looks at him.

Standing, Skye spreads her arms wide. Her cheeks shine red and I have never heard her voice so loud or shrill. "What about the people inside the Norm? If we destroy the AI what happens to them? Isn't anyone going to think about that?"

Next to me, Dat shakes his head and mutters, "She's talking like we can destroy the AI."

Dat is not wrong—we still have no real plans, but I am starting to have some ideas.

Wolf glances at Skye and nods. "We can help them. If the AI is no longer here, there is no reason Techs cannot learn to live in the Outside."

Staring at him, Skye slowly shakes her head. "And if they don't want to? We're talking about taking away their home." Her voice drops low. "My home." Skye looks close to tears. I can't believe she still thinks of the Norm as a place she might live, but she has memoires I don't. To me the Norm seemed like a pretty berry that will kill you if you eat it.

Voice rise again, this time split between those who want the AI gone no matter what and those who think there may be value in moving into the Norm after the AI is destroyed. I'm not sure that idea is even possible—without the AI to control climate and all the functions can the Norm exist? I keep wondering if the Empties was once like the Norm, with a dome over it that failed. Or if the AI got rid of every other AI—that would be something Conie would do.

Holding up his hands, Wolf calls out, "Enough. This is no longer talk—this is noise. Like Lib, I will not tell you what you must do. The AI controls. Each of you in Tracker Clan must follow your path. You know law—law is to keep the clan together. But this is more important than law. This is about if we live or die. So I will tell you now, I follow Lib. Who follows me?"

Otter stands, as does Star, Hawk, Alis, Pike and Dat. A few more stand. I count twelve all together out of the clan, which is only thirty-five strong. Skye starts to rock herself and keeps glancing at Bird. Standing, Bird calls out, "I follow no one who wears gear from the AI. I will only follow one who wants everything from the AI made into dust." She turns and walks out. Eight follow her, but I am not certain of their number for I can't finish the count before they leave.

Komodo stands then. "There is Big Hunt Clan beyond the mountains. Will some go with me?" A few swap glances, but no one stands to go with Komodo. He stalks from the room and I have no idea if he really plans to try and leave Tracker Clan to find another clan.

Looking around, I also have no idea if those who are still sitting and undecided will be a help in taking down the AI.

*   *   *

That night, I just want to sleep. The meeting leaves me exhausted. I crawl under my fur and pull it over my head and let my thoughts spin away.

Soft voices wake me. Across a still empty sleeping room, I can hear Skye, her voice low, say, "I didn't know."

Peering out from under my sleeping fur, I can barely make out Skye's pale hair. She has her arm over someone's shoulder and a flutter of ribbons in the moonlight next to Skye tells me it is Bird.

Bird's voice shakes and is thick, as if she is close to tears. "It's almost like he's haunting me."

"You're sure it's Raj?"

Cold washes over my skin and my heart seems to stutter. What does Bird mean Raj haunts her? Is he like a spirit? Croc sometimes tells stories around the evening meal and the fire about how spirits can come back if they feel they must be avenged or if they still have things they must do in this world. I've never experienced such a thing and never believed him, but Bird seems to believe in many unseen things.

Bird's ribbons flutter as she nods. "I think he's in trouble and reaching for help."

Skye's face seems to pale. "Is he…dead? I mean, Lib said she came out of the room with the AI and he was just…gone. The AI probably recycled his body."

"Forget what Lib said." Bird's voice sharpens. "Lib left him to the AI, but Raj isn't dead. And Lib still doesn't know every person matters. Raj is alive. I can feel him. I know."

I wonder now if Bird has been in the smoke that is supposed to give visions. Does she use it to try and reach Raj? Does she try to dream of him? Does she hate biogear so much because the smoke makes her react to the biogear?

"I don't think that's fair to Lib," Skye says, her tone firm. "If Raj wasn't there in the next room, Lib couldn't save him. Not if she had drones and Techs after her and the AI trying to kill her. But if we can save him now, we need to know where he is."

Bird lets out something between a sob and a sigh. "I don't know. I don't know the Norm. I just see blue and long, square tunnels. I keep trying to get Raj to show me more but I can't reach him. He can only cry out. He shows me metal boxes and things I don't understand."

Skye's voice drops to something soothing. Bird's soft sobs answer her murmurs. I pull the rug back over my head, but my heart is beating faster.

Raj is alive—Bird has seen him in visions. And the long, square corridors mean the AI has him."

At last I have an idea where the AI is holding him, but it's not good news. I think the AI has Raj with her in the AI's control core.

Chapter Twenty-Three

The next day Wolf wants to see the Norm before we make our plans. He picks a small group to go out that night and we spend the day getting ready. I can't risk my biogear not working—or making me ill—so I bring only parts of it that I can use without strapping on the full pack. I have a hand-held communication noise jammer and a screen that might work for me. When I don't wear my biogear pack, both Wolf and Alis give me long looks, but I just shrug and say, "I'm trying something new."

"This really the time for that?" Wolf asks.

I just shrug again.

We head out with Crow and Alis on one AT, and me and Wolf on a second AT. The ATs hum over the hard-packed ground. Rainy season seems to be late—very late. We leave the ATs hidden in a patch of tall bushes at the bottom of the ridgeline between us and the Norm and I have to scramble after the others. Alis and Crow move fast and easy. Their biogear lets them swing up over boulders and climb sheer cliffs. I follow Wolf's path up the steep mountainside, and even that is hard without biogear. I'm left sweating and cursing Bird and her smoke, which has left me barely able to use any gear.

Reaching the top, we stretch out, bellies to rock that is still warm from the sun. The night air is cool on my back— I miss the warmth of my biogear and glance over to Alis. She tinkers with her biogear, adjusting the screen in front of her right eye and I see her adjust a small dish that amplifies sounds.

Below us, the Norm seems a huge, dark spot—the dome almost seems like a smooth mountain. Scabs dance around the base—and drones hover in place, guarding the scabs. Putting on my biogear screen, I adjust it and see a drone actually pick up a scab and take it high, to a spot where the dome seems to have a hole. The scab disappears into the square hole. Light flashes and the scab climbs out and slides down the dome's side, landing on the ground. It gets up and walks to its next task. A fall like that would break any human's legs.

Scanning the work, I try to figure out what they're doing —I still don't know. Is the AI making improvements on the dome's design? Or is she adding weapons? What is she doing?

Beside me, Alis mutters, "I can't get this thing to focus." She adjusts the sight that hovers over her eye yet again.

"Use the outer bevel," I tell her. "Just think about what you want. Don't fight your biogear."

Which is, of course, my problem. Ever since I breathed in the smoke, my body seems to only want to fight the biogear. The effects are wearing off, but far too slowly.

Wolf holds up a hand and says, "Listen."

I do. In the distance an animal's roar echoes. A night bird trills a warning—it knows we are here—and falls silent. The wind rustles brush around us and a small animal —a rabbit or mole, scrabbles over the rocks. And then I hear what Wolf must have heard—a distant beeping that no animal can make.

Crow glances at me. "That the scabs talking? We should try to get closer and—"

"And what? We have no way of knowing what the scabs are saying—or if they're talking to the AI."

Crow stiffens. A full moon is rising on the far side of the drone, spilling silver light onto the world. "We could try the communication noise generator—and you really have to find a better name for it."

Turning, Wolf fixes a stare on me and I tell him, "It's new. Untested." But an idea starts to form. "But Crow is right. Now might be the time to try one out." Wolf starts to shake his head, so I tell him, "Wolf, didn't you say you follow my lead now? We're running out of time. And...and I have an idea, but I need to know if the...the noisemaker works."

"You want to let the AI know we're watching?"

I almost want to laugh. "I think she knows already—or figures we are out here somewhere. And she doesn't care."

A flash of white as Crow smiles brightens the night. "We should make the AI care."

I hand my noisemaker to Crow and ask, "How far can you throw this?"

He weighs the box with its tiny power-source in his hand. "How far do you need?"

Pointing to the drones, I tell him, "Down there."

He gives a nod. Placing my palm on the noisemaker, I concentrate. The gear doesn't hum to life, but sits in Crow's hand, a dead black box. Waving to Alis, I tell her, "See if you can switch it on. Just...just think about the connection inside. You've seen it. Picture it in your mind and give it the order to switch on."

Even in the moonlight, I can see her mouth pull down. "Me? Seriously?"

I wave at her again, and she puts her palm on the noisemaker. It starts to hum softly, sputters on, gives a click and is now steadily humming. But Crow doesn't even have to throw it at the drones.

The instant the connection noisemaker comes to life, the drones below us freeze as if caught by invisible hands. The scabs wander into each other and walk into the dome wall or start to walk in circles.

"Why are they acting like that?" Wolf asks.

"It's working," I mutter, breathing out the words. "They're lost—they can't hear the AI's commands, so the drones don't know what to do. They just wait for orders. And...and the scabs can't function—they're just doing core routines. They're wandering."

For a moment, I hold my breath. I hadn't expected the long range on the noisemaker. This is going to be useful.

The noisemaker whines down and dies—its power source is too small for it. Instantly the red lights on the drones begin blinking.

"We have to go. Leave that and get to the ATs," I tell everyone. I'm already running down the hillside when the first shot comes. The drones traced the noisemaker's signal. Glancing back, I see four drones blasting the black box into dust, their light beams cutting across the metal of the noisemaker like knives into soft fruit.

"Run," Wolf yells. He sweeps me up and half drags, half carries me down to the ATs. Rocks slid out from under my boots, but Wolf jerks me upright.

Crow and Alis get to the ATs first. Beams of red light dance after them—the drones have spotted us. Crow gets one AT going and Alis glances up. She uses her biogear weapon to fire back at the drone and hits one, but a drone targets her and she gives a cry as a beam cuts across her arm, leaving smoke and the stink of burning flesh in the air.

Reaching the ATs, I push Alis onto the one Crow is driving. Alis clutches her arm and is barely able to swing on behind Crow. "Get her out of here," I tell Crow.

The drones sweep down at us and without my biogear I'm not sure how to fight back. But Wolf is.

One drone turns and wheels after Crow's ATs, but Wolf pulls out a knife, aims a throw and his blade smashes into the blinking red light of the drone. It wobbles and spins, unable to target Crow and Alis. Turning, Wolf grabs one of long, metal poles from the side of the AT we're riding. He swings in a wide circle, I duck and Wolf smashes the poll into another drone, sending it careening into the fourth drone. The two collide with the rock of the ridgeline and rocks fall down on them. Metal arms burst out from the drone's black skin and the drones claw at the rocks pinning them.

Wolf grabs my hand. "Come on."

He pulls me onto the second AT, gets it humming and we slip into the night. We can't head back to the tunnels and safety—not with drones following. Wolf drives like a rabbit on the run from a wolf.

Beams of light hit the ground to the left and right of us —drones following, hunting. And I don't have another noisemaker.

Something burning hits my shoulder and I bite down on a cry. My back and arm go numb. I clutch at Wolf with my other arm. The AT bounces over rocks and Wolf turns into a wide, deep cut left by water long ago.

Wolf brings the AT up out of the deep cut and back onto the flat lands and then turns sharply into a canyon. I hang onto him, pain now searing my shoulder Ahead of us I see the dust from Crow's AT. Wind whips my hair and sand bites into my face. I've never been on an AT going this fast. It jumps over rocks, lands hard, jarring my teeth, making me gasp. Another whine sounds, louder than even the wind in my ears.

Looking up, I see drones darting past us, heading to the front of the canyon. Looking back more drones trail us. They're going to try and block us in. We can't go back now

—can't go up sheer, rocky canyon walls—and if they blast those walls and block the path, we'll be trapped.

I close my eyes and press my face into Wolf's back.

I was wrong. I shouldn't have tried the noisemaker—it worked, but the power source wasn't strong enough. I need a larger power supply—or to hook it up to the solar panels that charge the AT during the day.

But I can't just give up. Wolf fought with nothing but a knife and a metal pole. I will do the same. I pull Raj's knife from my belt. Glancing up, I look for a drone to try and fight.

I can't see one. The sky seems black, dotted only with stars. Canyon walls block the moon.

Rounding a bend in the canyon, we come across Alis and Crow. Alis has her hand on Crow's biogear and leans against him. Wolf slows his AT and stops next to Crow.

I glance from Crow to Alis. She offers a tired grin and winces, and Crow says, "I asked Dat to put whatever you had in your biogear in mine."

I stare at him. "You have a noisemaker?"

He nods. "Couldn't make it work, but Alis did."

I shake my head and glance at Alis. Her face seems far too pale and I know if she passes out from the pain of her wound, she may not be able to keep the noisemaker working. Right now, too, it's using the power supply on Crow's biogear pack—but that won't last forever, either.

Wolf speaks the words I'm already thinking. "Let's not wait around to see how long this one lasts."

Crow nods. He turns his AT and Wolf follows as we speed into the low mountains, leaving tracks that lead away from the tunnels. We'll have to hide the ATs anywhere we can and walk back. My shoulder is screaming and I do not look forward to that walk.

But I have a plan at last for how we can get into the Norm.

*   *   *

We don't make it back to the tunnels until almost dawn. The moon sets and the sky is a pale gold when we stagger to one of the entrances. Wolf insists on stopping to bind the wound on Alis's arm. He also has ointment he puts on my shoulder that takes the pain away, leaving it just numb. Now I know why he always takes a pouch out with him with extra supplies.

Alis slides down the rope—her biogear leaves her able to do that. I stare at the rope that leads into the tunnels, but Wolf simply wraps his arm around my waist, pulls me against him and jumps down into the tunnel. I bite down on a gasp, but Wolf manages to catch the rope with one hand. We're left swinging in midair for an instant and then Wolf lowers us both to the ground. I want to cling to him, but Gazelle is here, along with Wind and Skye and Bird and everyone is staring at us.

Wolf gives the orders. "Get Croc. Drones hit us."

Pulling away from Wolf's hold—and not wanting to lose his warmth, I shake my head. "I can walk. Croc doesn't have to come here."

Wolf grunts and waves to me and Alis. "Then get yourselves to Croc. We'll talk about this after."

I nod—we have plans to make.

Alis and I stagger more than walk to Croc's room. He frowns at us and his stare sharpens when he starts to look at our injuries. He mutters about Wolf's messy bandage on Alis's arm, tells her to keep it open and gives her plant leaves to put on it, saying "It's a burn, but it'll heal well. No bone hit and no muscle." Looking at me, he shakes his head.

"It's a burn, too," I tell him.

Croc frowns and sorts through his plants and ointments. He pulls out something that looks a lot like the dried leaves Bird used to make her smoke. I hold up a hand. "I'm not using that."

Croc's eyebrows lift high. "Bird? She used this on you? Her smoke?" Face hot, I can only nod. Croc lets out a breath. "She knows a lot about plants—all the See Far Clan did. But she...she uses too much of the smoke. But she wants her vision." He comes over to me and shakes his head. "This is not just a burn. It's hit muscle and touched bone. It'll heal, but you were lucky it didn't go deeper and hit a lung—you wouldn't be breathing now."

I wet my lips and look up. Wolf stands in the doorway to Croc's room, his arms crossed. He is frowning. For a moment I think he will say I cannot go back—that this is too dangerous.

Instead, as Croc packs my wound and wraps it, Wolf says, "We need a new vantage point. And I want you to tell me about all the gear you have."

Chapter Twenty-Four

Croc tells me I need weeks to heal. I tell him we may not have that much time.

He gives me something to ease the pain, but I refuse that. So he gives Wolf the herbs for pain as well as ointment to put on the wound every day. "It's going to scar," Croc says.

I think of all the scars on Wolf's back and chest—small, white lines and two big ones on his side from a wild boar that nearly killed him on his first scavenge when he was younger than Dat. Dat loves to tell that story about Wolf. Now I'm really part of the Tracker Clan—we all have scars.

Wolf wants me to rest, but I know we need to talk. We head to the main room and find most of the clan there with food out. I'm suddenly starving. All of us eat, but we are still on water rations. My head aches from not having enough water—and from our encounter with the drones. Wolf seems to know that for he tries to give me his water, but I refuse. Instead I eat as much fruit as I can since it is wet.

Sitting in the main room with Wolf, I listen as he tells the others what we saw. Worry tightens his face, pulling at his mouth and carving new lines in his forehead.

When Wolf is finished talking, I glance around at those who are here—we have a few of the undecided clan members and all of those who will follow. I'm hoping they will all listen. A trickle of cold slips into my stomach.

I clear my throat and stand, still cradling my injured arm.

"Obviously, the AI doesn't want us getting too close. The drones and the scabs were clearly ready to kill us, but we have a way to block their communication. We also know the AI has limited resources—she hoards water and materials. The only thing she wastes is humans—so that's the only resource the AI must feel she has in abundance."

Alis pulls a sour face. "And what does all that mean?"

"It means the AI is more dangerous than ever. It also looked as if she's getting close to being finished with the Norm. But I think we can literally glitch that program."

A few of the clan swap glances, but Alis nods as if she understands where I'm headed.

"If the AI needs scabs and drones to finish reworking the Norm to leave, then she's not going to want us going after them. That means they're perfect for a diversion."

Crow shrugs. "Maybe."

I shake my head. My shoulder is throbbing, but I do my best to ignore it. "No maybe. We need one group to head out and get close to the Norm on the ATs we have—the drones and scabs will go after them. Then a second group goes in—we'll get drones and scabs not knowing which group to go after. We have a noise making device—it creates interference between the drones and scabs and the AI's control. We'll need three—one for each group luring the drones and scabs into a chase, and a third to use right at the Norm.

Frowning at me, Skye says, "You're thinking of going in."

I nod. "The scabs have to remove panels off the dome to work on the Norm—that leaves a gap we can use to gain access."

"But...are you inside the Norm then, or inside the dome?" Dat asks.

"Inside the dome, but once there, we can find an access panel to remove to get inside."

"That or blast a hole," Crow says."

I shake my head. "No—that'll draw the AI's attention as well as Techs to make repairs. We have to go in without seeming to create a problem to be repaired. But once I'm inside the dome, I should be able to make a connect and get access. The trick will be to keep the AI focused on activity outside the Norm—that's our key for getting in."

"And once you're in?" Skye asks. She sounds worried and she tugs on the end of her pale hair.

I almost admit I haven't thought that far ahead—but I have. Once inside, I need to find the AI's core, find Raj and then disconnect the AI from her power source. All that sounds easy, and I know it may not even be possible. But I have to try.

Wolf saves me from having to answer by asking, "How long until you have those noisemakers ready?"

I glance around the hopeful faces. I want to go right back out again, but Alis's face is pale from pain, and everyone looks tired. Crow's face is brown with dirt from the chase we just went through. I look at Wolf and tell him, "Give me two days."

* * *

Dat insists on working on the noisemaker—he made one for Crow so he can increase the power. I want him to at least try. And Wolf wants me to rest. "You can't think if you're falling asleep."

He's right, but I hate to waste a moment. I head to the sleeping room. This early it's empty. Exhausted, I curl up on top of my sleeping fur, but my shoulder burns and as soon as I close my eyes, the images come.

Drones flying after us, beams of light streaking the sky.
Bodies strewn over the ground—Lizard's sightless eyes.
The AI, wearing Dr. Sig's face, smiling at me.

But she's not real. She's not!

I jerk awake and realize I have been sleeping and dreaming. Sweat slicks my skin. My heart is racing and my hair is matted to my forehead. Sitting up, I glance around, but the room is still empty and sunlight filters down through the holes in the ceiling. I'm shaking and thirsty, and worried this is the vision Bird promised me—that everyone will die.

I fall back against my sleeping fur and lay on my uninjured side. Sleep won't come. But I don't want it—I don't want that dream again.

A few deep breaths and I'm able to wipe the sweat from my face. It's time to get to work.

Heading for the Gear Room, I have to wonder if the AI tries to reach me when I dream. Is she trying to draw me to her? So she can kill me? It's a scary thought, but maybe the AI wants me frightened.

It's hard to think when you can't even breathe.

I find Dat struggling with trying to get the noisemaker to work with a bigger power supply—he glances at me and admits he blew the circuit for Crow's noisemaker already. After telling him to take a break, I bury myself in the biogear.

For once, feeling queasy around the biogear is good—it takes my mind off my dream and off the pain in my shoulder.

*   *   *

It takes me three days and three more nights to get all the noisemakers done. I have two portable ones, and one integrated with a biogear pack. Croc's ointment works better than I thought it would. The wound still hurts and I have to keep it wrapped, but now it only bothers me if I move to fast or bump it.

Each time I try to rest, I dream of people dying and of the AI.

I almost talk to Bird about the dream to ask if she thinks it's a vision. But Bird avoids the Gear Room, and I only see her at meal times and there are too many others around then for me to talk. The clan almost seems optimistic about the plan I laid out—I don't want to ruin that by making everyone think we have to fail because a dream says we might.

This is just fear.

I keep telling myself that.

Wolf sets the attack for tonight. The first group goes out early to get the ATs and get into position. I've left the details to Wolf. Tiger and Crow are in charge of that group. Crow seems unhappy not to be going into the Norm, but I know we need to keep that group small or the AI will figure out our plan.

Pike and Star lead the second group. Croc doesn't think either Alis or I are healed enough to go out, but we don't listen to him. Bird won't go with either group—and a few of the clan are on her side because both groups will have biogear and the noisemakers with them. In a way, I'm relieved that some of the clan is staying behind. The rest of us might die trying to stop the AI. As long as we succeed, it will be worth it.

But I keep thinking about how Bird kept saying every life matters. I still don't understand that. The exchange of fifteen of us—for that's how many will go out—so everyone else can life seems a good equation. Am I not seeing something that Bird sees?

There is no time to talk with her about it, for night falls and it's time for the last group to head out—it's just me and Wolf.

In the Gear Room, I head over to touch my biogear. I can touch it now without throwing up, and sometimes it works. I don't know if it'll work tonight, but this pack has the third noisemaker.

Deciding to take the biogear, I swing it onto my shoulder but don't connect it. Not yet at least.

I head to the exit, tension knitting my stomach and leaving me jumpy. I'm halfway down the hall when I hear something behind me. Wolf waiting for me, his pouch slung over his shoulder. He glances at the biogear I'm not wearing and then at me. He gives a nod as if he's satisfied about something.

"Ready?" I ask.

He gives a nod, but I have to tell him one more thing. I put a hand on his arm to make him pause and then I look up into his eyes, hoping he'll understand. "Raj is still alive. Or at least Bird thinks so. If he is, we have to save him. Because it's my fault he's there."

Wolf frowns. "From what you told me, it wasn't your fault. Raj knew the risks. Probably better than you."

I shake my head. "If Raj is where I think he is—being held by the AI near Conie's core, he may have learned just what we need to know."

His frown deepens. "How to shut down the AI."

I nod. "Bird keeps saying everyone matters—maybe Raj is really the one here who matters most."

He takes a deep breath and releases it. "Let's find out if he is."

The two other groups have the ATs, so Wolf and I must walk to the Norm. The night is cool and Wolf knows how to avoid the most dangerous big animals that hunt at night. We head not to the ridgeline where we watched the Norm, but the canyons and the path that leads to a platform where there have been the fewest drones and scabs working. At least until now. I keep feeling something is watching us, and Wolf keeps pausing and glancing back, holding up his hand for me to be quiet.

The third time he does this, he also pulls me into the shadow of a large boulder. We wait a few moments. My breath seems too loud to me. I want to rub my injured shoulder, but I hold still.

Soft boot steps squish into the sand, and Wolf steps from the shadow. From behind him I have to lean around to see that Skye stands in front of Wolf now. She wears a scavenge pouch slung over her shoulder and a water skin. She stops and stares at Wolf, her eyes wide and the moonlight making her pale hair seem silver.

"What are you doing?" Wolf demands.

Skye glances at me, but I'm not going to defend her. I edge closer to Wolf—I'm with him. Chin lifting, Skye mutters, "You might need my help."

"Might?" I ask. "You sound like you know something we don't." She tugs on her hair and I notice a ribbon has been braided into a few strands. "Bird told you to come?"

She shrugs. "I won't go back. I'll keep following if I have to."

I worry now, because Skye has made it clear she doesn't think the AI should be destroyed. Is she here because Bird sent her—or is she here to make sure we don't ruin her chance of returning to the Norm some day?

Wolf turns to me. "We don't have time to take her back. Can't leave her tied up or she'll get eaten."

Skye shoots him a look. I don't see a choice. If Bird had a vision, there's a possibility we need Skye. And I would rather have her where I could watch her and not following us into the Norm and going off on her own.

With a glance at her, I tell her, "Stay close and do what I tell you. Or I will have Wolf tie you up and you can get eaten."

Chapter Twenty-Five

We reach the Norm before the moon rises, but just barely. Moonrise is when the plan is set to start. The scabs and drones seem to work night and day—or at least they do as far as we have seen before this.

"Where are we going in?" Wolf asks.

Now I really want my biogear so I can use the screen. Slipping the biogear off my shoulder, I shake it out and start to swing it on. I have to hope it will work.

Reaching out, Skye snatches at the straps and stops me. "You can't."

"We need to get a closer look, but we can't get any closer just yet."

She shakes her head. "Bird said you shouldn't. You have to see your path and have your vision."

Wolf glances from Skye to me. "What vision?"

I wave away his question. Skye tugs on the strap. "There is no mistaking a vision—you haven't seen your path. And I...I'll use the biogear."

I stare at her. "How do you know it'll work for you?"

She glances away, but looks back and admits, "Dat showed me."

I'm annoyed and even more worried now. Skye was there with Bird's smoke, too, but somehow she has recovered and I haven't. Was there something else Bird did to me that wasn't done to Skye?

Then I remember the white clay I used on my face. It wasn't the smoke that somehow changed my body so I became ill when I tried to use the biogear—it was something in that clay. Skye didn't use it. But if she can use it now—it seems a better option than my trying and failing.

The moon is almost fully up in the sky—clearing the horizon is the time to start the diversion and we need our entrance by then. I give up my hold on the biogear.

It is obvious Skye hasn't worn the biogear before now. I have to help her with the straps. She bats away my hands and the wires connect into her. "What am I looking for again?"

I glance at Wolf. He is frowning hard, but he lifts a hand as if to say 'let her help.' Turning to Skye, I point to the Norm. "The drones and scabs are about to be lured away from the Norm—or most of them will be. Look for an access panel—we need a large one close enough to the ground we can climb in."

She stares at the Norm. The screen comes up in front of her right eye—that's good. The biogear is working for her. She seems to be searching and finally nods. "I think I found an entry point."

Just as she says that, moonrise is done and the wine of drones fills the sky. Glancing over, I see the ATs as just specs and columns of dust. Crow's whoop carries to me on the night air. A group of drones breaks away from the Norm to follow the ATs.

I count to thirty—the second group should go now.

They do.

ATs charge the Norm and then spin away, heading for the flatlands. More drones take off after them. Scabs mill around the base of the dome, or slump, as the AI focuses on sending drones after our two diversion groups.

"C'mon," I tell the others. We run for the Norm. Skye gets in front of us—the biogear giving her more speed that either Wolf or me. She heads for an open square that's been left by the scabs. I eye the scabs and the remaining drones and tell Skye, "Think about activating the noisemaker." She glances at me and I tell her, "Just do it."

Stopping, Skye closes her eyes. I don't know if the noisemaker is working to cut off all communication between the AI and the remaining drones and scabs. It's got to give us a little time.

As I hoped, just inside the open panel, wires and connections weave around the space between the outside of the Norm's dome and the inside. There is just enough room to slip inside. Wolf looks like he's about to say something, but I reach for a connection railing. Slapping my palm against it, I slip into the connect.

Connection: secure.

Needles seem to prick against my palm and instantly I'm inside the virtual world. The cool blue walls do not seem as comforting to me as usual. Yellow and red tinge the edges of the long corridors. I turn from the rows of cabinets and call up a screen and begin my search.

Code dances in front of me—lines and lines of code. I need specifics.

It seems to both take forever and only a heartbeat to find what I need. Looking at the code, I see just how much work the scabs have been doing. This is major modifications to the structure of the dome—and it is not just a dome. The Norm is really a giant sphere, extending miles underground and connections everywhere. And the AI hasn't just been hoarding water and food—she's been extracting raw minerals for manufacturing. She's been getting ready for this for a very long time.

And then I find it—*Drone program.*

The code to hunt takes a moment to isolate. I work a loop around—the drones will start to hunt, hit a cancel hunt line and loop back to start. This will put them in circles. It's a temporary fix. The AI will find my adjustments at some point—or one of her Techs will—and do a restore, but with the noisemakers on, the drones won't be able to be updated. This will leave them scrambled.

I need to leave, but I have one more thing to do—a delay. Going back, I dive into the scab programming. It's not much but I set a delete command and alter priorities. Scabs will now take apart much of their work. That will at least buy us some more time.

My skin prickles. I jerk away from the screen to search the blue corridor around me, but see nothing. No sentinel firewalls. Nothing. Heading back in, I keep working, but I can't shake the feeling I'm being watched.

It can't be the AI. Conie would stop me from this hack if she knew I was here. I finish the rewrite as quickly as possible and disconnect.

I blink and bat away the wires surrounding me. I'm back in the space between the outside skin of the Norm and the inside. It is no longer a dome to me—it's a sphere. One that can leave this world behind someday. I glance behind me to see that Wolf and Skye are watching, and both look worried.

"Well?" Wolf asks.

"We've got some time," I tell him.

"Now what?" Skye asks.

"We head into the Norm. Find a way in."

For a moment, she stares blankly at me. I want to rip the biogear off her and put it on, but I have no guarantee it will work for me. So I tell her, "Use the screen. Think about access inside the...here." I wave into the area where I stand. "The Norm has to process materials. The AI hasn't just been taking water, it's been mining, and it has to recycle waste and air and most of that goes on in here—in the space between the Outside and the inside where the Norm is so nice and pretty."

Skye steps into the open space. She's still wearing the screen over her eye and scans the area, finally looking up. "There. We have to climb."

Wolf has trouble getting into so small a space, but he manages and we make our way up, climbing up wires. My shoulder starts to ache, and now I wish I had some of Croc's herbs to chew for the pain.

When we reach a platform and I bend over, breathing hard, my shoulder burning. Skye is not even sweating and I wish even more that I, too, had biogear on. Even Wolf makes the climbing seem easy.

Skye waves to the end of the platform. "There," she tells us.

We pick our way through the wiring. It is getting darker, the light is almost like in the tunnels, with patches of dim moonlight slanting in through any access panel that has been removed to allow work. Connection railings appear every now and then and I have to resist touching them to make a connections. We need to get inside the Norm. And I have to trust Skye really is leading us there.

Wolf's shoulders are brushing against the metal framing. Sometimes we have to climb wires. Other places have platforms that scabs or Techs must use for repair work. And if Techs and scabs get in here, there must be an access from within the Norm—the AI would need that once they're in space.

Skye hesitates and glances around. "I've spotted what looks like an access tunnel, but you're probably not going to like it." She glances back at us. "It's for waste."

Wolf shrugs and I wave Skye forward. She leads us down to the edge of a platform and then to a place where there is a long drop. It looks like a wide, square hole. I'm relieved to see it seems to be dry, or at least I don't see the glint of moonlight on any liquid. "I thought you said this was for waste?"

She lifts a hand and waves at her screen. "This is pulling up the names of things—this is listed as waste. But maybe the scabs changed things, because a lot of this doesn't—"

The platform we're on tilts, sending Skye tumbling down into the opening in the piping. Skye gives a shout. Wolf grabs me around the waist and grabs a wire to keep us from falling. I call out to Skye and my voice echoes.

I look to Wolf. His face is taut and his grip is slipping on the wire he holds. We're going to follow Skye.

"Keep your arms tucked tight," Wolf says. I nod and take a breath. Wolf swings and lets go. I fall straight down, warm air rushing past me, and land boots first into warm water.

Mouth and eyes clamped closed, I kick for the surface. I come up sputtering, splashing in the water. Wolf lands next to me, but doesn't sink and I realize there is a floor or something that's slippery and slimy and I can stand. The water—or whatever it is, for it stinks—reaches only to my hips. Streams of light dance around me from tiny glowing gobs strung up everywhere.

I look for Skye and find her standing next to a man who holds tightly to her arm. And when I glance at his face, I have to fight not to cringe.

Chapter Twenty-Six

Wolf has followed me and now stands beside me, but where is Skye?

The man's face is covered with the ugly puckered scars that comes from burns. Hair stands up in a dirty clump on one side of his head. But his most disconcerting feature is that he has one seemingly normal eye, and one that is a flashing red eye.

Like on a drone.

I suppress a shudder and glance away—and see others lined up along what seems to be the wall that holds this liquid. Disfigured faces stare at me and Wolf—and their bodies are even worse.

One man has scab legs instead of his own. A woman's side looks made of the skin off a drone, and yet another has a drone arm instead of any human arms. They all look as if someone cut them apart and put them back together with mechanical parts. This is far worse than biogear.

They're both intriguing and horrifying. They make my insides twist, but I hold still and say nothing, for some of them hold weapons taken from drones. One drone weapon points at Skye's head.

Next to me, Wolf says, "Let her go."

The man holding Skye glances at Wolf, but looks back at me. Like all the others, he wears what looks like a much-patched tunic and pants that a Tech might wear. The material is worn to a dull gray—whatever color it once had is long faded. His one human eye is a dark brown. His mouth tugs down at the corners, making the scars seem even worse. "You're not Rejects. We were waiting for Rejects we could scoop from harm's way." His voice is surprisingly sweet, soft and almost soothing.

Wolf sloshes forward and stops when the man—the Reject?—presses his weapon to Skye's temple. "We're only passing through." Wolf spreads his hands wide.

The man tears his stare away from me to look at Wolf. "There is no passing through. There's only the Norm."

I step forward, the liquid pulling at my legs, my clothes sodden and starting to stink. "There's the Outside."

A ripple of murmurs echoes. He shoots a harsh look around him, and the murmurs subside. He fixes his mismatched eyes on me. "You don't look like a Rogue."

"You know what Rogues are then? I am one—I'm Tracker Clan. All three of us are. But I was a Glitch."

The man narrows his human eye. The red eye blinks faster. "Impossible. Glitches don't come back. AI send you after us?"

I glance at Skye, then at Wolf. Finally, I look back at the man. "We're here to stop the AI."

Skye frowns, but with a weapon pointed at her, she keeps quiet.

He laughs. "If that's the case, we have common cause." He releases Skye and jumps into the water, slogging closer to me. Beneath his scars blue lines cross under his skin— and light surges over them. Those lines are wires.

"Name's Mech. You're in Rejectland, so come with me," Mech says and waves for us to follow.

The other Rejects seem almost to vanish. When I look around us, they're all gone and I have no idea where they went.

Mech leads us out of the waters and into dry tunnels similar to those made by the Tracker Clan. But these tunnels are metal and exposed wires hang from the walls and ceilings.

I stay close to Wolf and Skye huddles between us, her arms wrapped around her and shivering, her teeth chattering. I don't think it's that cold.

Mech takes us to a smaller room with metal chairs. It seems decorated with scrap pieces—bits of drones, copper wire woven into the shapes of trees or plants. One woman, tall and slim with a shaved head and a tunic that hangs off her, lingers. Half her face looks made of silver metal. Mech nods to her. She scowls back but steps into the room and closes a door behind her.

It has been a very long time since I last saw a door—in fact, I last saw one within the Norm.

"Sit," Mech says, waves at a metal chair and sits down in the biggest chair in the middle of the far wall. He glances a few times at Skye, as if he's fascinated by her.

I glance at Wolf. He glances at one of the chairs, crosses his arms and leans his shoulder against a wall where he can keep an eye on both Mech and the metal-faced woman. That seems to me the wrong attitude to take with a man who still holds a drone weapon, so I take a seat opposite Mech. Skye goes over and stands next to Wolf.

Mech smiles at me. "Before we do any real talking, need to be sure."

"Sure of what?" I ask.

The woman comes over to me and puts her fingertip on my arm. A sting pricks my skin. I jump up and Wolf is instantly beside me, holding the woman's arm in his hand. She smiles, and Wolf suddenly jumps back, jerking his hand away. The woman waves a hand, and Skye gasps and slaps a hand to her heck.

Turning on Mech, Wolf demands, "What was that?" Still rubbing her neck, Skye tries to hide behind Wolf.

Mech shrugs. "Just a nanobit. It'll find any connect to the AI in your system and sever it."

Wolf's eyes narrow. "You put gear inside us?"

Mech glances at him. "Won't live long. Has enough power to do its job that's all. AI has every Tech under control. So, got to hit you with a nanobit. If you don't have anything from the AI in you, the nanobit's harmless."

"But if we have something from the AI in us…not so harmless?" I ask. Mech just keeps smiling. A cold that has nothing to do with my dripping skins that I wear races down my spine. I've wondered if the AI had a connection to me—now I will find out. "How long does it take?" I ask and rub my injured arm. The water has seemed to make my shoulder ache even more.

Mech glances at the girl who put the nanobits into us. She pulls a face, but only the non-metal side of her face moves.

Mech looks back at me. "Done. Now we talk."

Chapter Twenty-Seven

The AI doesn't have any literal connection to me.

Relief washes through me. The dreams I've had are just dreams—or maybe something the AI implanted in me to make me think the AI cannot be defeated. Conie wanted me giving up even before I started anything. I sit down again, and Mech puts his weapon away, tucking it into a pocket hidden somewhere in the side of his tunic.

"That's Med." The woman stands as far from us as she can. She, too, has the blue wiring beneath her skin and light slicks over the wires in what must be energy bursts.

Wolf rubs at his arm and I can tell he doesn't like the idea that gear is now inside him. I…I am oddly fine with the idea and the reality. I introduce everyone and ask, "What exactly is this place?"

"Told you…Rejectland. We're the AI's failures—the spliced humans she tried to graft gear onto. Most of us went into the recycle bin, but some of us got out and started pulling others out before they got sliced up into compost." Mech grins. "Been living under the AI's nose till we find a way to stuff her code up her virtual butt."

Skye lifts a hand, showing the biogear she wears. I don't know if it survived the water. "Biogear you can't take off," she mutters.

"You can take that off?" Mech says. "Fancy that. AI wanted us wired for link up directly to her without troubles most show."

"Trouble?" Wolf asked.

Med speaks up. "Seizures. Headaches. Nightmares. Disassociation. Techs spend too much time in the system, can't take it no more."

Mech nods. "AI tried to fix that with us. Part human part grafts and wires and lots of machine." He waves his hand to indicate his scars and gear stitched into his body. "AI didn't count on us saving ourselves."

"Why didn't she put you in the Outside?" Skye asks.

He laughs. "Turn us Rejects loose with gear we could come back and use on her? No, AI thinks us dead—sent to be made into compost for the soil. We've been letting her think that. Now, how you thinking about stopping her?"

Leaning forward, my damp clothes clinging to me, I tell him, "I have some ideas, but we need to get to the AI's core. And we're looking for a friend who'll be there—held by the AI."

Mech's eyebrows lift high over his one good eye and his red eye. "Won't be successful in that."

"We still have to try. The AI has plans to destroy this world."

"What and take the Norm with it?"

"No—take the Norm somewhere else."

He stares at me, glances at Skye. His stare lingers on her. Finally, he looks at Wolf and back at me. "We all seen the scabs working. Wondered what they were doing. Been working around the clock. Have to run and hide from them. Well, you want to do AI harm, guess we'll just have to help with that."

My eyes narrow suspiciously.

"You're going to help us?" Wolf says. "Why?"

Mech stands. "'Cause the AI ever finds us, we'll be compost soon enough. And anything that does the AI's plans no good is good by me. Come on." He leads us out of the room. Several of the other Rejects stare at us, suspicion in their glares.

I follow Mech, and Skye and Wolf trail behind, with Wolf keeping an eye on everyone around us.

As we walk, Mech says, "Been a long time since we saved any Rejects. Been thinking AI gave up on making more of us. Med thinks AI's got plans to wash us out of Rejectland. Med's good on hacking for data mining."

I glance back to see Med following us. She trails us like a shadow, the metallic side of her face reflecting the lights that line the Reject's tunnels.

I'm suddenly not so sure the AI gave up on anything. Techs are not entirely human—that's why Glitches can still connect and hack the AI's systems. What if the Rejects were experiments—and then the AI moved on to something else?

Glancing around, the biogear seems almost—a step toward this. I shake my head. At least we can take off the biogear. But this still leaves me

Mech glances at me. From this side I can only see his good eye and I think he was once handsome. "Data we get on the AI is only bits. Can't go into the Norm—we stand out and AI has sentinels lined up to try and sniff us out. Figured with all the scabs working AI had plans."

"She does. She's getting the Norm ready to go into space."

Mech stops and stares at me. "That what your data on her says?"

"That's what the AI—what Conie told me."

Mech snorts and starts walking again. "Sounds like the AI. Never mind costs, AI gotta have her plans."

Skye moves up between us and glances at Mech. "If we succeed, the Norm may be destroyed."

Mech waves her away. "Norm without the AI might be a place to live. Not a place to hide."

We head into a square room with metal cabinets that line two of the walls.

"This is where we keep all the goods," Mech says. "We take what we can from recycling and get more with reclaimed water and algae. Some of us even raid the Norm."

"How do you raid?" I ask."

Mech grins. "Most can't pass for a Tech, but some can." He waves a hand at Med. "Put on right clothes and cover up the parts and she can pass."

He goes to one of the tall cabinets and opens the door. He pulls out a Tech's tunic and offers it to Skye. "You'll look good in this."

She smoothes a hand over it. "I haven't worn cloth in… in I don't know how long."

Mech glances at Wolf. "You're bigger than most Techs. Best slouch and don't say much."

Mech begins to pull out more clothing, handing pieces to each of us. I run a hand over the tunic and then the pants.

The fabric is incredibly soft—it reminds me of the tunic I had on when the AI put me into the Outside.

"Got face paint to slap on your skin. Techs have pale skin—you're all brown as Rogues."

Skye asks, "What about my biogear?"

Mech frowns, but tells her, "Get you a coat to put over it, or carry it like gear you gotta fix. Techs do lots of fixing and carrying stuff. We always see them doing that."

Looking up from the fabric, I ask, "We're just supposed to throw on some new clothes and expect them to believe that we belong?" I ask, a little skeptical. It's still a better plan than I have—which is to hide behind buildings and avoid interacting with anyone—but it doesn't sound very safe or secure.

Shrugging a little, he nods. "Not a lot more we can do except offer you a mirror."

"What's a mirror?" Skye asks

But I already know the answer—it comes into my mind at once, a lost memory found. "It's gear. Lets the wearer blend."

Mech nods. "Told you AI has control to everyone. Glitches had it pulled." He waves at Wolf, "He's never had one. Mirror picks up what Tech next to him has and shows it back so you blend. Now dress, then we look how to get you close to the core."

Taking off the wet skins is a relief. We all change quickly. Skye bundles her biogear into a bag that Med gives her. Once I have on a white tunic, pants and flat shoes made of fabric, I ask Mech, "What about the mirrors?"

Skye turns to me and offers me her hand. "Isn't it pretty?"

She wears a thin, silver bracelet on her left wrist. It's perfectly smooth. If I angle it right, I can see my own reflection and, in that moment I understand why it's called a mirror. "This is an impressive…assuming it works."

Med hands me a mirror and I slip it on. A thread-thin wire connects it, slipping under my skin with a small spark.

Mech taps my wrist. "Keep it on. Gear like this cost us hours and hours. Med made it work.

Wolf tugs on his tunic and frowns. Coming over to me, he gives me a look and I know he's thinking we're putting a lot of trust in these Rejects.

Staring back at him I try to let him know it's not like we have a lot of choice.

Wolf's tunic and pants all seem tight on him. His shirt isn't much better in fit, but it looks better. The muscles in his arms, chest and thighs stretch the fabric.

Wolf tugs at the tunic, and Skye giggles. She clamps a hand over her mouth.

Med offers Wolf a mirror, but Wolf just stares at it. Taking the mirror from Med, I fasten it around Wolf's wrist. His skin is warm against mine, his pulse beating strong against my fingertips. "You have to wear it. Or you have to go back."

Wolf frowns, but doesn't move.

Letting go of Wolf, I look at Mech. "Okay, what about where we enter the Norm?"

Mech takes us to another room, this one with a map of the Norm drawn onto one of the walls. It's amazingly detailed.

He shows us our current location and then points to the outer and lower systems that link the Norm's maintenance areas. "This is your best path in. It's part of the oldest section of the Norm."

"There are old parts and new parts?" Skye asks.

Mech nods. "You think this was built in a couple of years? No, the AI's been enlarging, enclosing, altering for a long, long time. Parts of the Norm have worn out. The AI just closes them off. That's where you go in. Don't let Techs see you going in. Remember, what a Tech sees, the AI sees."

Skye nods and smooths her hair. Her eyes have a glitter to them that I haven't seen in a long time, as if she's happy. Wolf just frowns and tugs on his tunic. I wonder if he's going to be even more trouble than Skye—Wolf's never been inside the Norm, but both Skye and I know how to act like Techs.

"Once you're in, stay on the paved paths. Techs follow rules—they follow paths. The AI moved the core not long ago. Don't know why—just did. Used to be in the Norm's hub, but AI shifted functions over to the green zone."

I am not surprised by this. The AI wouldn't want me to find the core again—as I did once before with Raj. Now that I blend in better this time, I'm less worried about getting where I need to go. My worries lie elsewhere.

There are things I need to figure out from the AI. Things that I think she can answer—and that no one else could. But how do I ask them while Wolf and Skye are with me? And if I spend too much time trying to get the answer, will I lose the chance to cripple the AI?

I'm not sure I can take that risk.

"One last thing," Mech says, turning from the map on the wall. He waves at my wrist. "Mirrors are just masks. Works with Techs who don't know your face. That works for Rejects, but two of you were Techs. That means any Tech sees you who knows you will know you don't belong. Avoid anyone who you would recognize—that's your biggest risk."

Chapter Twenty-Eight

Stepping into the Norm is an odd thing—the last time I was here, the AI sent every Tech after me. This seemingly peaceful place became a death trap. Once again, the Norm seems quiet. It is night, or at least the dome—the top of the sphere that holds the Norm—shows a black sky. A few lights glitter in the surrounding buildings.

This place is like the Empties, with tall buildings and wide, paved paths between them. But it is green like nowhere else I have ever seen. Trees and grass dot the spaces between buildings. I pull in a breath. The air always smells odd in the Norm—like it is tainted with chemicals and something else. The Outside smells of dust and of electricity before a storm and sometimes of rain. But here —the Norm always smells the same. The Norm always looks the same.

After looking at Mech's map, the route to the green zone where the AI relocated her core is clear in my mind. My heart is pounding and I want to hurry, but a Tech would not be in a rush. Gulping a breath, I try to slow my pace and I tug at Wolf's hand to make him slow as well. Skye has already fallen into a steady pace, and looks around us with a smile curving her lips.

Skye glances around, as if she's taking in every sight, every building, every blade of grass, every leaf on every tree. There is a look in her eyes that has me worried. She misses this place in a way I never can. My only memories of the Norm are those that I experienced with Raj.

Two Techs come out of a building and walk toward us. Next to me, Wolf tenses. I put a hand on his arm, but my heart is pounding. The Tech passes us as if we are not even there. The mirrors are working—even for Wolf.

It seems to take far too long to reach the green zone. Mech pointed out the building that now houses the AI's core—it is a small building, but Mech said most of the structure is underground.

Outside a very plain door, I stop and glance at Wolf. "You two need to stay here." Wolf starts to protest, but I cut off his words. "This is what will happen. Once I connect and slip into the AI's core, she will know I'm here. If you two are with me, she can use both of you against me."

Wolf shakes his head. "How?"

But Skye touches Wolf's arm. "Lib is right. If we're out here, we can still act like Techs. We're hidden. We can help her escape, even blend back into a crowd of Techs."

I'm surprised that Skye realizes this, but she suddenly hugs me and whispers in my ear, "Find Raj." She lets me go and backs up a step.

Wolf still looks unhappy, but he glances around us and then up at the dome, which is starting to brighten, meaning the day inside the Norm is beginning. "I give you five counts of one hundred. After that, Skye puts on the biogear and we come after you. Even if we have to start tearing down walls," he tells me fiercely.

I don't doubt that he'll try to do just that.

Five counts of one hundred. It's not a lot of time, but I hope it's enough.

Smiling at him, I nod and reach for the door. Before I can open it, he grabs my arm and spins me around. He pulls me against him. My eyes widen in surprise. Then he leans down and presses his mouth to mine. The kiss is quick, but urgent. It's not a goodbye, but a promise to come back. That he'll be here when I do.

He nods at me then, and I'm still breathless. My limbs feel weak for a moment, but I force myself to go to the door. I drink in Wolf's features once more, and then I slip inside.

For a moment I stand with my back pressed to the door. It feels hard and chilly. I had thought it was made of wood, but now I know it is cold metal. My heart is beating fast and my breaths come even faster.

I expect drones or something…some form of resistance. But I see only a narrow hall that stretches away from me and slopes downward. Deep blue colors the walls. The floor is bare. Lights line the edges of the ceiling. I start to walk down the hall.

My palms are slick with sweat. The hall curves and keeps sloping downward. I break into a slow jog and at last see a door—a single door.

Walking up to it, I put my right hand flat against it. The door slips open as if I am expected. But no one is there on the other side. Nothing tries to stop me from going deeper.

Sweat pops up on my upper lip. Wiping it away with the back of one finger, I keep going.

Inside the room, a connect railing runs along the far wall. Screens also appear along the walls at regular intervals. Everything seems new—it's all gleaming. This is so unlike anything in the Outside, or even anything where the Rejects life.

And Raj is not here.

But he must be. I know the AI has him somewhere close. Or at least I think I know that. The way Bird described her vision sounded like how the AI's core looks, which means Raj must be here.

Walking over to the connect railing, I wipe my hand against my thigh and then wiggle my fingers. Am I ready to connect? I have to be—Wolf is outside counting down the time I have.

I wrap my hand around the railing and the connect stings my palm. Taking a breath, I close my eyes.

Connection: Secure.

Opening my eyes in the virtual world, I see the long, blue corridor that is the AI's system. I expect sentinels—firewalls—to spring up or block me. Instead, this place seems peaceful—quiet. Far too quiet.

This deep in the AI, I find no cabinets—this isn't a place to store data. However, blue lights dart past, flickering and traveling. These are the AI's thoughts. She is busy with something.

But Raj has to be my priority. I think about a screen and one appears for me. Turning to it, I begin a search. Code scrolls past me—but something isn't right. I keep scanning, searching for a sign that Raj is here or at least nearby somewhere in the Norm. There must be a trace of him within the AI's core—she knows where he is.

I scroll past more code, shift my thoughts to look not for Raj but for anything abnormal, anything to be kept in stasis or imprisoned.

Instead of a location in the Norm, more code streams past me. I study it—but the code isn't finished. It's also not part of the AI's system. I know Conie's code—it has a cold logic that runs through it. This is wilder—leaping about with its directives.

Halfway through, I know this has to be something Raj created. The code speaks like him—with a sarcastic edge and a dark humor and a purpose that suddenly stands out.

It's a virus.

The code, if released, will slowly infect and replace the AI's core systems. I have no idea when Raj created this, but I see why the AI has imprisoned his code—it has a failsafe within it so if the AI touches it, the virus, even half finished, will activate. It might not be able in this current state to destroy all of the AI, but it would severely damage the AI's ability to maintain a fully functioning Norm. The AI would never be able to take the Norm away from this world.

Hope flares up within me. The AI must have kept Raj alive to try and force him to undo this—or at least to delete it. She isolated the code and Raj, but if the code is still here, Raj must be, too. Conie would destroy Raj the second after he wiped this code. Raj has Conie in a no-win situation—she can't kill him but she can't let him go either.

Was this why Raj wanted to come back to the Norm—to finish this? Was this how he intended to correct the AI?

I don't know those answers.

I also cannot access the virus. If I could, I could complete Raj's work and activate the virus. This would destroy the AI, or cripple it.

But the isolation around the code is tight. This isn't just a firewall, but layers and layers of additional code to hold the virus in a set of memory where it cannot touch anything else—and no one can touch it. However, there must be a way to access it for otherwise it could not be deleted.

I start to search for an access point into Raj's virus.

Instead, I find core functionality.

This code seems…benign. The lines jump past almost faster than I can read them, but it is soon clear that the original code is meant to preserve the human race. Routines create functions to learn the needs of the people, and sort out viable compromises between wants, needs and survival. There is a forecasting routine as well, meant to look ahead to long-term planning The self-learning system is impressive, and I'm drawn to reading more. This can't be Conie's core system—nothing I come across is designed for control or for discarding people as if they have no worth. If Raj saw this—knew this—no wonder he thought he could repair the AI.

Slipping out of this program, I skirt around, looking for the back way into Raj's virus. That is still my best chance to shut down the AI. I follow a small thread that leads me to what I hope is an access point. I catch a few lines of maintenance and at last find a way into shutting down the isolation around the virus by telling the isolation code that Raj's virus is not really Raj's—it's code Conie created.

The trick works. The isolation falls off the virus and it starts to slip free, but Raj's virus is only half finished. It can only damage the AI's function. I need to complete his work.

The virtual world around me starts to fade as Raj's code begins to work its way into various systems, but I cannot let it go yet—Raj's virus must be finished. Sweating now, I grab the last lines and work quickly, adding lines and commands, wrapping my mind around the code, forming new lines and releasing them to follow the rest of the virus.

This has to work. This has to work.

I keep thinking those words over and over as if this will force my plan to be a reality.

I am almost done with the last lines when the screen in front of me vanishes, leaving me touching nothing.

I go cold, chilled straight though. This shouldn't happen. Not if Raj's virus really worked.

But what if this is a trap?

You can't stop me, Lib.

The voice echoes inside my own mind. Conie is here. The AI. She's still alive. My heart jumps with a hard thud and I look around. I still don't see her, but now I'm not sure if there really was a virus created by Raj. Was that a trick? Was any part of this real? Did the AI just want to lure me here and keep me busy so she could deal with the clan members outside before she dealt with me?

A wall in front of me glows to life. It displays a view out into the Norm. I look out into the green zone. The dome-sky is bright now, glowing a pale blue, but I can only see edges of the dome-sky for the view is from above, looking

342

down onto trees and grass and buildings. And onto where Skye and Wolf wait for me. Wolf is pacing. He digs one hand into his hair as if he's frustrated, and Skye has dropped the bag of biogear and is shaking the door by the handle, trying to open it. They've been locked out. I want to yell at them to run, get away, blend in with other Techs, or head back to the Rejects who can get them out of the Norm.

Something black with wings flies into view to the left and then yet another one comes into view from the right. I've never seen such things. They look like huge, black birds, but they have red, electronic eyes, and their wings seem fixed in place. They are like the Rejects—mechanical things, or like birds made from parts and gear. The red eyes seem fixed onto Skye and Wolf

I want Skye to put on her biogear—to use it. Use anything to fight the black things headed for them.

Turning, I shout to the empty, artificial space around me, "No. You have me. Let them go!"

That is not a recognized command, Lib. Threats to the Norm must be eliminated.

At last, Wolf seems to sense the danger. He turns and looks up. He takes a step back and reaches for the knife that should be at his belt, but which isn't there. Techs don't wear knives. Skye glances up as well, but she still does not reach for the biogear—she seems not even to think of it. The metal bird to the right turns and dives and weapons shoot out of the tips of its wings. The screens go black. Fear washes through me.

No, this can't be!

"I have to get out of here," I mutter.

Willing myself out, I break the connection.

The blue of the artificial word vanishes. Blinking, I stagger a step. I am back inside the AI's core, in the room with the connect railing and access to the AI. I turn and take one step, heading for the door. But something makes me look up and I have to blink to focus my eyes on the world around me and the shadowy figure in the doorway.

The figure—what looks like a Tech all in white—steps forward and light spills over Raj's face. He's always been thin, but he seems thinner now. His face is no longer a deep brown, but his skin seems washed with a grayish ting. He

344

wears the white tunic and pants that every tech wears, and instead of lean, wiry muscles, I can see his wrist bones. "Raj?" I can't focus on anything else—just my hammering heart and Raj.

He smiles at me. Walking over to him, I wrap my arms around him. He is so very thin. "I'm sorry…I should have looked for you. I should have stayed and found you."

"It's okay," he says, but he doesn't hug me back. "You did the right thing."

Stepping back, I can only shake my head and say, "I left you behind. I should have found you and taken you out with me, but how…what happened to you? You weren't in the room outside the AI's core when I came out, and I had drones after me, and then—.

"There is not enough time to explain everything. Come." He turns and strides out of the room, seeming to think I will follow.

It's so incredibly good to see him, but something isn't quite right. He's dressed like a Tech, but he is stiff, and I don't hear that tone in his voice that I used to hear. But he has been inside the Norm for some time—something has happened to him.

I follow him and he glances back and says, "Conie has new sentinels she can put outside a connect—so she can send them into the Norm. Once she regains control, she will send scabs and drones after us. We must move fast."

Hurrying past him at a jog, I tell him, "Wolf and Skye are outside—did you see them?"

He shakes his head. I have to jog down the hall to keep up with Raj's long stride. I burst out of the front door and stop. I'm half terrified I will find Wolf and Skye lying dead on the ground, or struggling against those metal birds that have to be the new sentinels made by the AI. Instead the area outside the AI's core is empty. Glancing at Raj, I ask, "Where's Wolf? And Skye?"

Raj turns to the right and takes my hand. He strides along the paved path, pulling me with him. "We have to move."

I glance back once more, looking for Skye and Wolf, but see no trace of them. Jerking away from Raj, I tell him, "We have to find Skye and Wolf. I won't leave without them. I can't do that. I won't do that. The AI may be willing to throw people away—no one really matters to her. You saw her core code—she may have started as a program to save people, but she's made the idea of people a general concept. She's lost her path. Everyone has to matter—or no one matters."

Raj stops, turns to me and frowns. He tips his head to one side as if he's thinking—but his brown eyes seem to glaze over. My skin prickles and I suddenly am worried about Raj. He doesn't look right. Straightening, he looks at me again. "If the AI has them, I know where to look."

He turns and starts to walk again. I follow him, wishing now that I had kept his knife, no longer really certain this Raj is the one I knew. But I must find Wolf and Skye, so for now I will see where Raj is leading me.

Raj follows the rules Mech gave to us to behave like any Tech. This leaves me tugging on the hem of my tunic and glancing around us. I have seen no other Techs, so why does Raj think he has to act like one? Glancing up at the sky, I don't see the metal birds either, and I don't hear the hum of drones or scabs.

The quiet unnerves me. So does Raj acting like a Tech. I keep remembering how Conie took control of the Techs the last time Raj and I got into the Norm—she made the Techs into her tools. And Mech said that all Techs have something inside them that lets Conie track and control them. Is Raj under the AI's control?

Maybe he's just behaving like this so he can survive— the exact same thing I have been doing.

As we walk past buildings and down the paved paths, I can't resist asking, "What happened to you, Raj?" I keep my voice calm, even, though my breath comes in short bursts and I want to turn and run and leave this place.

Raj shakes his head. He turns a corner, walks up a narrow path and stops in front of a building that looks like all the others. How does anyone know where to go here? He waves for me to follow and puts a finger to his mouth to tell me to be silent. Without waiting to see if I will follow him, he opens the door and steps inside.

Glancing behind me, I debate the wisdom of following Raj. But this might be the place where the AI kept Raj— and where the AI now holds Wolf and Skye. I also let Raj's virus loose—the Norm might be struggling because of that virus. That might be why everything is so quiet, why no Techs come out. Maybe the metal birds carried Wolf and Skye here. I have to go inside to find out because I cannot leave without them.

Fingering the mirror—the metal bracelet Med gave me —I take a breath. I tug off the bracelet and hang onto it in one fist. It is useless now. Then I step into the room.

It is like making a connect. A long, blue corridor stretches out in front of me. Dim strips of lights line the ceiling. Glancing around I do not see any cabinets—no screens appear. And yet this is so much like the AI's artificial world that it leaves me wanting to turn around and leave. I have to remind myself that I have not made a connect. I glance at Raj. He seems to be waiting for something. Footsteps echo in the empty, blue corridor.

I freeze.

A woman steps into the corridor, coming in from a shadowed doorway, and now I can see there are a dozen such doorways—tall rectangles—that open into the corridor. The woman stops and smiles. I stand there, shaking my head.

The woman wears a white, flowing dress, and I recognize her oval face and the high cheekbones. Her smooth, dark hair is pulled up and wound into a knot. Long lashes sweep down as she blinks. Her eyes are kind and very blue—but they no longer glow. Not like they do in the artificial world.

But how did Conie get out of her artificial world and into this world? How is it she has a real form. Or is this really Dr. Constance Sig, the woman who created the AI?

Chapter Twenty-Nine

I want to turn and run. I want to shout questions at her. Instead, I cannot seem to move. I'm trembling. The AI was created long ago so how can Dr. Sig still be alive? Swallowing, I wet my dry lips and ask in a voice that shakes, "Who are you? You can't be Dr. Sig."

The woman smiles and walks over to face me. She moves stiffly in a way that reminds me of the Rejects and the ones that had gear instead of legs. "Dr. Sig died a long time ago. That is the difficulty with a body. It ages. Wears out. It is a poor design. But the essence of Dr. Sig remains."

"What do you mean essence?"

"Brain wave patterns. Data stored in memory. Those can be retained. The body has an electrical essence that can be captured and rerouted."

I glance at Raj. He stands to my right, and the…the AI that has taken physical form stands in front of me. For a moment I consider turning and running, but Raj is very tall.

He can easily catch up with me and I fear he will only drag me back here.

I cannot trust him—he is a tool of the AI now.

Glancing back at the AI, I pull in a breath and stand straighter. "This is why you experimented with blending gear into people."

She gives a small nod. "A start. The blend of mechanical and biology was a first step, but it proved—inefficient. The body still aged and the blending did not always last. Those attempts were rejected and new plans made for a better mechanical option with only some biology inside."

"Like a drone." I mutter the words. I know the drones use organs inside—biology of some kind. I had no idea the AI could use that on a human-type of being. Glancing at Raj, I realize this may not even be Raj. Maybe the AI has created her own Raj—a mechanical being with some of Raj's mind inside it.

Looking back at Conie—I cannot think of her as the dead Dr. Sig—I ask, "Why did you bring me here?"

Conie's smile broadens, but it does not warm me. The expression is only a lifting of her mouth. Her blue eyes do no change. "You have proven an unusual survival rate and drive. Calculations show a value in reintegrating such learning."

"You went from wanting to kill me to…wanting to know what I know now?" I ask. I glance around me again, searching for a way out. If I can't outrun Raj, I need another plan. I need to keep Conie talking. The metal of the mirror bites into my palm, but I am not certain yet what I can do with it to get away from here.

And I have to know what Conie has done with Wolf and Skye.

Conie tips her head to one side as if studying me. "Your…biogear…you call it that." She waves at Raj. He leaves through one of the doorways and returns to the blue corridor with the biogear Skye was carrying. "This is a better step in the direction I was trying for. Your knowledge of such things needs to be reintegrated for future improvements in extending human life beyond what it is currently able to sustain. Travel between planets requires either many generations or extended life spans. Optimum forecasts show a greater efficiency if humans can be converted to energy power to remove the need for water and food fuel."

Now I can only stare at Conie, horrified. "You want to make people into you—you want them to be made of gear."

"No, more like you. I made you—a blend of biology and gear."

For a second, I have to clench my eyes shut. I was made? Created? This is my family. I'm a thing—not a child that was born. Opening my eyes, I stare at Conie. "I don't believe you. You're an AI that lies."

"Belief is not required. You have become important to future plans, Lib. Forecasts show you are key to saving the human race."

I take a step back. "What are you talking about?"

"Initial programming to find the Glitches was successful. However, you altered your programming. Your task to find Glitches, and therefore reveal Rogue locations

for those that had connected to Glitches proved…
unsuccessful."

I shake my head. When Conie talks, I can hear a slight
clicking in her voice. And I start to realize she cannot resist
a question—she must be programmed to always answer. "It
doesn't matter what you wanted me to do—I don't do what
you want."

Conie's expression flattens. "That is where you are too
much like me." She smiles again. "Like mother, like
daughter. You share much with Dr. Sig—her DNA is inside
you. Once you proved you would not fulfill your purpose,
elimination seemed the best option. But now new options
are in the forecasts." She waves at the biogear.

The biogear is saving my life—I almost can't believe it.
But I don't know what Conie means by reintegration. I
don't think that can be a good thing. Does she plan to take
me apart? Will she do to me what she did to Raj? Take
parts of my mind, take my memories? What will she leave
behind?

Hands fisting, I consider the very real possibility that the
AI is telling the truth. She made me—from Dr. Sig's DNA,

from part of her stored somewhere. The AI is my mother. Or—more accurately—my creator.

But then I think of the Rejects. The AI made them—and threw them away. She named them failures. But they have not allowed the AI to define them. And Conie said it herself —I changed my own programming. I can learn, just like Conie. I have become something other than she made me.

Glancing at Conie, I ask, "Why can't you just go away with the Norm and leave this world to the Rogues and Glitches?"

Conie's smile drops away again. It is as if all she knows is how to lift her lips to fake a smile. She may think she has parts of Dr. Sig's mind and maybe some of the real woman's memories, but the AI does not understand the complexity of being human. Not in the way I do. "You have spent time with Rogues and Glitches. They are uncontrollable. Far too random. They bring in a rebellious nature and genetic deficiencies. Things that will ultimately cause the destruction of the human race. Probability studies show they cannot be reintegrated."

I glance at Raj and back to the AI. "Did you reintegrate Raj?"

Raj answers me, as if—like Conie—he cannot resist a question and must answer. As if it is core to his programming. "Raj is a Glitch. Reintegration is not possible. However, new assembly requires testing."

I gasp, appalled. "You're not Raj. You're...like her." I wave a hand at Conie. "You're a thing with some of Raj's memories and his mind." Turning to Conie, I ask, "What about Skye and Wolf? Where are they? Are you trying to build new versions of them? Make them into gear you can better control with just bits and pieces of bodies so you can think they're still human?"

Conie's smile widens. "For the good of the whole, we must sacrifice a few."

Her words wash over me and I remember thinking the same thing myself not so long ago. Didn't Bird warn me of this thing, how sacrificing anyone becomes a dangerous way to think?

Am I as much a monster as Conie?

Glancing from Conie to Raj, I realize the only way I can escape is to get to the biogear. I don't know if it will work for me. Maybe I'm even wrong to try and use it. Maybe it makes me too much like Conie. But the biogear will make me faster and stronger. I can use the screen to try and find Wolf and Skye. I have to get to it, but as I edge closer to the biogear, Raj moves too, as if to block me. I have to find a distraction—just as the clan was a distraction outside the Norm.

Taking a deep breath, I search for another question to ask. Something to force Conie and Raj to have to think about answering me—I have to keep them focused on their need to answer me. "Why go into space? Why leave this world?"

Raj stops, and Conie answers. "Long-term planning shows this world's sun will expire in ten thousand years. Additionally, resources to create a better human—one with longer life spans—"

"You mean humans that are more like drones," I tell her and ease closer to the biogear.

Conie tips her head to one side. "No, drones are far too primitive and limited. New humans require advanced resource that can be better found in space."

I step closer to the biogear, but I hope it looks as if I'm trying to ease over to one of the doorways. It does, for Raj steps as if to block any potential escape into one of the doorways.

Glancing over his shoulder, I can glimpse into the doorway. Inside, gear that is unlike anything I have ever seen seems to fill with room. This gear—it really is partially organic and partially something else. Instead of wires, tubes with flowing liquid connect what seems like floating screens. Light dances around the room, traveling on its own in globes. I blink. This is far more advanced than anything I have ever known. Has the AI been making improvements—or is there another answer?

Turning to the AI, I ask, "Where did Dr. Sig get the ability to develop an advanced AI? Why do you think you can find better resources in space to advance the human race?"

Canting her head to the side, she studies me. "You know the answers, Lib. But I blocked access to those memories. You did not need the knowledge to find the Glitches, but with reintegration those memories will return."

"Where?" I ask again. "You have to answer."

For a moment, she almost seems to struggle with trying not to answer. Her lips flatten and her eyes almost start to glow. But then her smile returns and she says, "The discovery of alien technology on the second manned Mars mission proved vital to Dr. Sig's work."

"Alien," I whisper. I can't help but repeat the word. The AI is partially alien. A faint memory stirs at her use of the word technology. I have always thought of gear—that has been the word for anything mechanical. But this new word —yes, technology. Something far more advanced than gear.

Conie steps closer to me and I step away. She holds out a hand. "Come, Lib, you must reintegrate."

I back up, angling my steps to get me closer to the biogear. "So alien technology helped create you—create what we have? Why do you want to go into space? Do you know of another viable planet?"

She shakes her head. "No, however, humanity will not survive an encounter with advanced alien races. Probability studies show an eighty-five percent likelihood that additional aliens will follow up with visits to this area. Best chances for the survival of the human race is to leave no trace that we exist. We must leave nothing behind."

I shake my head. "Dr. Sig could not have wanted that. She didn't make you do to that."

"Of course she does. I am her. I am what is left of her. Dr. Sig created my basic programming, but the technology for the dome, for our survival, wasn't advanced enough. When environmental disaster struck, the government informed her they had something to allow cities to be saved. Dr. Sig integrated the alien technology into me, but an accident occurred. The only way to save her was to pull her consciousness into my system. The bioelectrical fluid that powered the alien technology allowed such a connection. It has taken a great deal of work to reverse engineer the alien technology and recreate a form for her, but I have done so at last so she lives again."

I can't understand everything she's saying, but I really don't care. I'm almost in reach of the biogear.

"When are you taking the Norm away and destroying this world?"

"Reworking of system finishes in four solar months."

I glance at Raj. He still stands in front of one of the doorways. Can I get the biogear on and fastened—or will he just grab me and stop me? Can I distract him with the mirror in my hand somehow? Looking at Conie, I tell her, "Why do you really think the aliens will come again? They haven't been back—not since before the time of Dr. Sig."

She smiles. "You will understand with reintegration." She touches my hand, energy washes through me, and images flash into my mind.

An explosion sends waves of sand and fire into the air. Plants shrivel into ash. The rocks are scorched black and then they are blasted away to nothing more than dust. Dust swirls into the air, sweeping across the Outside. The blast engulfs the Norm, shattering the dome. In a flash, everything vaporizes.

Nothing is left. Nothing but fragments of debris.

Pulling in a harsh, painful breath, I break away from Conie. This is what she fears will happen if the aliens return—this is why she fights to save the Norm, but only the Norm.

My lungs burn. I'm shaking. The images Conie tore loose from my memory—or just gave me—seem to echo. Everyone dead and the world gone. I stagger and sit down —right next to my biogear. But I can't pick it up.

Looking up, I see Conie. Anger washes through me. "You did that. You created that image to try and convince me you are right! But it's all a lie. You say it is probable— that doesn't mean it really will happen!"

Conie says nothing, but Raj shifts on his feet, as if he is the real Raj, and says, "That is the future that's coming. We have to leave. We must not leave a trace of where we are going."

"No," I whisper. "No." Sitting up, I hunch over the biogear, and put a hand on it. The power light glows softly.

Raj steps for me. I throw the mirror bracelet into the room I glimpsed with the alien technology. Both Raj and Conie turn and Raj heads into the room to retrieve what I threw in there. I slip on the biogear while Conie is watching Raj. My fingers shake as I get the straps on. The wires connect. But will it work?

Standing, I tell Conie, "I'm coming back for Raj. For everyone. And for you."

Conie turns and looks at me. I slam a fist into her face. She goes down, her skin peeling back to show metal. My hand aches. Conie starts to call out to Raj—to the fake Raj she made—but I slam my fist down on her face again, pulling off the skin that feels like skin. I don't want her to wear that face. I don't want her to think she is human. She isn't. And she doesn't belong in this world. Using the strength from the biogear, I tear off her legs and arms, leaving her body oozing reddish-brown fluid and jerking. I smash my fist into the spot that was her mouth—I don't want her using that voice—Dr. Sig's voice—to tell more lies.

I smash her eyes and tear off her skin, leaving her looking more like a scab with a smooth, black metal face, and a lump that is what is left of her mechanical body. Getting up, I glance around, half expecting an army of Techs or drones to swarm me.

Instead, Raj stands in the doorway to the room with the alien technology, watching me. "What are you doing, Lib?"

Standing, I face him. "I came back for you—but I came back for the real Raj."

"I am Raj."

"Are you? The real Raj wouldn't be helping the AI. The real Raj started a virus—he wanted to fix the AI, not become part of her lies. The real Raj hated lies. Is there anything of him inside of you?"

His face blanks, but then something of Raj's personality seems to twist the mouth into an expression I do recognize. "I'm here...I'm...still...here." He growls the words as if he's struggling to get them out.

The biogear is on and working right now, but I can feel the power fluctuating. I may not have much time. Stepping closer, I tell this other Raj, "If you are Raj, then you know better. You need to be Raj—you need to finish his work. I know his code...your code. Raj really did start on a virus that would affect the AI—at least you can slow her down."

"I am not. I am progra—" He bites off the words and stares at me. "I'm not Raj?"

"Be Raj—if you are him, find that part of him that Conie put into you. Raj is here and still alive. You can help him. You can help everyone."

Raj glances into the room behind him. His head tips and he looks back at me. "Rogues and Glitches are converging on the dome. I have…access to outside views. You…must…go." The last words come out stuttered as if he had to push them out.

"Raj?"

He glances at me. "I will do what I can."

He turns and walks into the room with the alien technology. For a moment I don't know what he plans, but then he smashes a fist into one of the floating screens. The glowing light darting around the room converges on him. He doesn't cry out, just swats at them. I start in to help him, but the room brightens and a flash and loud noise sends me flying backwards. My back hits a wall. When I can open my eyes, I see the dome's sky through a hole in the building. I can smell something burning and smoke chokes me, leaving me coughing.

Dragging myself to my feet, I get up and stagger out, leaving the mechanical Conie's flopping body and whatever of the Raj she created. I fear he is gone. I can only hope the real Raj is still here somewhere just as Bird thought—that whatever Conie does to put someone into a mechanical body is not fatal.

Outside, the world seems chaos. Techs wander the streets, seeming without the AI's control. I don't know if Conie put all of herself into that body she made, or if she only put a version of herself there. Drones fall from the sky, land and roll to a stop, then launch up again to fly in seemingly random patterns. Scabs stagger around, bumping into Techs and walls.

Flipping down the screen on the biogear, I search for Wolf and Conie. Techs are easy to identify—I can pick up the same device Conie uses to track them. So I just have to look for anyone who doesn't have that. Behind me, an explosion shakes the building, knocking me to the ground.

Pushing back up to my feet, I run.

The biogear makes me faster than the Techs, faster than drones or scabs. I head back, retracing the path that brought me to the green zone. Scanning the crowds in the street I search for Wolf and Skye.

The biogear gives a hiss and stops working. The wires retract leaving me without my speed or extra strength. Yanking it off, I give in to the last thing I know what to do.

Putting my head back, I give a howl like one of Wolf's long wolf-like howls. I give another and a third. And then a hand grabs my arm, spins me around and I find myself in Wolf's hard grip and pressed tight against his wide chest. "I thought I'd lost you," I mutter.

He holds my shoulders and pushes me away from him.

Glancing over his shoulders, I see Mech and Med. Mech glances around us, grinning. Med is frowning. "Where's Skye? What happened to you?" I ask.

Mech's grin widens and he lifts a hand to show me a metal bird in his grip. "Was keeping an eye on you. Good thing, too. Got us some new parts. Not a bad day, but time to head out of here by the looks of it."

He is right. The Techs no longer seem quite so disoriented or panicked. They have all frozen as if the AI is resetting and trying to take control of them again. The drones and scabs also hold still, off for the moment, but if the AI is moving back out of the body she built and back into her core, she will regain control.

We have bought time—or at least the artificial Raj has bought us time. The AI will have to recover from the damage the artificial Raj created. And maybe the real Raj's virus will also slow her.

"I found Raj," I tell Wolf. "But it wasn't really Raj. The AI made a thing that looked like him."

Med starts to jog away from us. Mech says, "Got Skye holding the door for you. Best go." He runs after Med, and I realize he must have artificial legs for he is very fast.

Wolf grabs my hand. Around us, the Techs are starting to move. "Come on."

We run. I keep glancing back. Without the biogear I have no way to find Raj—and I fear he is dead. But I have promised Conie I will be back—but I am not coming back until I know exactly how to destroy her. But I leave knowing more than I did—and knowing that I can become more than a match for Conie.

If Conie made me, and if I am also part of Dr. Sig, then I am part of what created the AI. That means I can also end her.

Skye waits at the access panel that leads back into the area between the dome's walls. She waves us to move faster. Med slips inside. Mech stands next to Skye, waving for us to run faster. Around us, the drones' red lights blink on.

Wolf pushes me ahead of him, and Mech just about throws me into the dimness of the inside of the dome. It smells of wires and oil in here. Someone—Wolf I think—grabs my hand. His white tunic is torn, and my clothes are soon stained with smears of dirt and grease.

Mech leads us through the wires and I see daylight framed in an open square of an access panel that leads to the Outside.

I stop next to the panel and glance back.

I did not get what I wanted this time into the Norm, but I am leaving with new information. I don't know what I will do with it—but I have changed. I know this. I can learn. I can grow. I may be the AI's creation, but I am not under her control.

I choose my own path.

Glancing out into the Outside from inside the dome's walls, I think how this world could be green again. The AI withholds the rain, changes the weather, and tries to kill everything outside the dome. But she went from wanting me dead to wanting to know how I keep surviving.

I am going back to my real family now—to the Rogues and the Glitches. And every one of us matters. Every one of us must live, so all of us can fight the AI.

Mech stops Skye with a finger to her arm and whispers something to her. It might be good luck or something more private, He takes her hand, squeezes it and lets go. I nod to Mech and tell him, "The AI's hurt. She may lash out. Or she may just have a hard time recovering. I don't know what it will be."

He smiles. "Rejects been living a long time. We'll go on living."

I nod. "We may need your help again."

He shrugs. "We may need you, too. Come visit." With a wave, he disappears into the wires and darkness of the area between the walls.

Wolf helps Skye climb out. She gives a last, longing look back and then goes. Wolf takes my hand. "It'll be a drop."

I nod. "I can manage," I tell him. And even without biogear, I know I'll find a way.

Outside, I hit the dusty ground and slowly stand, my hands still aching from where I smashed it into the AI's artificial face. I hear the whoops first—clan yelling and screaming. I fear someone is dying. Instead, ATs surge out of the sand and dust swirling into the air, churned up by the tires.

The clan who'd been outside for a distraction came back. They swing iron pipes, smashing the frozen non-functional scabs to the ground and striking at the drones' black shells. The air is filled with their yells and the sound of metal on metal. Crow skids to a stop on his AT. "Climb on," he calls out.

I do. Pike rides up and Wolf slips onto the AT behind her. I see Skye jump onto the AT that Dat drives. We tear away from the Norm, heading out before the AI can regain control over the drones and scabs.

Leaning against Crow, I close my eyes, but I keep seeing the images the AI showed me of the world smashed into nothing. I have to lift my head and open my eyes, and I think instead of how this world could look—green as the Norm, lush and strong.

It doesn't have to be her way—I can choose my own path.

It is almost sunset again before we reach the tunnels. Everyone is being cautious—we change direction four times, leaving tracks at the end that seem headed for the Empties. We hide the ATs in a deep canyon with thick overhanging rocks, and walk back to the tunnels. I am glad to see we have only injuries—some bad burns, one broken arm from an AT crash and Crow damaged his biogear. My tunic is now dust-colored, not white, and I cannot wait to burn it and put on skins again.

Climbing down into the tunnels, I see Bird waiting for us. She scans the faces of those returning, and I see the look in her eyes. She hopes to see Raj with us.

I walk over to her. I can't tell her I saw Raj because I didn't but I stop in front of her. "I had my vision, Bird. I see my path." I glance at Crow's biogear. "And that's not my way. You were right. I needed to learn that. And I still have a promise to keep about going back for Raj."

Bird nods, her ribbons fluttering. She turns and walks away, her head down. I glance at Wolf. He pulls off his tunic and wads it up. "We have plans to make—and stories to tell." Looking around, he stands a little taller. "We meet around the fire so everyone can have a talk." He speaks as if to everyone, but his eyes are on me. I figure he wants to know what happened to me. I'm relieved the Rejects looked after Wolf and Skye—or maybe Mech was looking after Skye really, and Wolf was just an afterthought for Mech. Either way works for me.

Glancing down at my hand, I flex my fingers. A cool wind drifts down to brush my cheek from the hole that leads out of the tunnel. The rope in and out sways. The evening breeze is here.

Looking up, I watch the first star appear in the sky. The AI wants to badly to go to the stars—is that the alien technology inside Conie pushing her to do this? She wants to make every person into a thing—a mechanical being that can live forever.

This is why each life must matter—life, real life, is so short and fragile.

Glancing over at Wolf, I give him a nod. I know my path.

It's the one that will lead me to finding a way to protect my true family—the Tracker Clan.

The End of The Empties

The Norm, Book 3 out

Early 2017

Sign up to Ramona Finn's mailing list to be notified of new releases and get exclusive excerpts!

Sign up at <u>https://forms.aweber.com/form/81/231664481.htm</u>

You can also find me on Facebook at

<u>www.facebook.com/ramonafinnbooks/</u>

38091719R00214

Made in the USA
Middletown, DE
13 December 2016